VENI I CAME VIDI I SAW AMAVI I LOVED

... AND AN ANGEL IN SILVER SHOES TAUGHT ME REAL LOVE

AF663308

notionpress.com

VENI I CAME VIDI I SAW AMAVI I LOVED

... AND AN ANGEL IN SILVER SHOES TAUGHT ME REAL LOVE

PRADEEP SHARMA

notionpress
.com

Notion Press

Old No. 38, New No. 6
McNichols Road, Chetpet
Chennai - 600 031

First Published by Notion Press 2016

ISBN 978-93-86009-65-4

This book is dedicated to:

The angel in silver shoes—you know who you are.

You also know that it is only because of you that this book has been written.

There are no accidents.

–Master Oogway, *Kung Fu Panda*

Contents

Acknowledgements

I would need to write a whole book of Gratitude if I were to acknowledge all the people spread across the Globe whom I am grateful to in my life, especially my family, extended family, dear friends, colleagues – past and present, associates and every person I ever interacted with, who helped me shape the way I am, which led me to write this book. Since I am not writing that book, at least not yet, here I would like to mention a few people who have influenced / helped / motivated me with this book.

Arpita – Thank you!

Kalparupa – When you asked me to write a book not knowing that I was already writing one, I sought your help with certain ideas that I incorporated in the book without letting you know. Thank you for helping out!

Meghna Pant – Thank you for holding the writing workshop at the time when I needed it the most. As you rightly said, it was 'serendipity'!

Ruchika – Thank you for reading the entire manuscript twice before designing the cover. Not sure how many designers would have done that for me! Your feedback on the book was very encouraging and suggestions were priceless!

Simi – You were the first person to mention that I could have a book in me, and that too more than a decade ago! I promised you back then that if I ever wrote a book, your name would be there in the 'Acknowledgements', so here it is! I drew motivation from what you said. Thank you!

I would like to thank the entire team at Notion Press, especially Ann, Gracy and Mridula. Thank you for being patient with me and putting up with my craziness and unrealistic demands - which you did your best to meet! This book would not have come out the way it did if it wasn't for you guys!

Lots of love and Gratitude!

Prologue

"Hello. Is this a book publishing house?"

"Yes, it is. How may I assist you?"

"I want to write a book. Will you publish it?"

"You said you want to write a book or that you have written a book? Not sure if I heard you right."

"I want to."

"Oh. Authors generally approach us only after they have written any book, not before. Have you written anything earlier?"

"Hmm…Yes, I wrote essays when I was in school, around twenty years back."

"Oh, okay. Well, we need to go through the quality of your recent writing to see if we can publish your work or not. Please start writing, and email samples of your work to us. Our Editorial Board will review it, and we will then communicate our decision to you."

"I see. And how many words do I need to write for a proper book?"

"There is no fixed criteria as such—however, we expect a minimum of around thirty thousand words."

"Oh! Okay, I will get back to you."

Sangharsh was sorely dejected after the telephonic conversation. He didn't know *her* beyond three words. How could he write thirty thousand? And she didn't know him at all.

Even if he wrote about whatever little interaction he had had with her, which was miraculous in its own way—the very reason why he wanted to write—it would still not be enough.

An accidental meeting of a new-to-Mumbai boy with a Mumbai girl on a suburban street, where he falls in love at first sight within a third of a second, but doesn't tell her. A few days of interaction over text messages, which she ended but with a "promise." No contact after that. He left Mumbai, but kept with him the only thing she had given him on the day they met. He carried it with him EVERY SINGLE DAY. Wherever he went in the world, it travelled with him. He just couldn't forget her. After seven years, he relocated to Mumbai again and miraculously found her. Did she unknowingly "invite" him when the time was right to honor her 'promise'?

After a few days of interacting with her, he sabotaged his chances by sending her something. Did he unknowingly push her away from his life even though every inch of him wanted to be beside her? The conflicts between the conscious and unconscious levels of both their lives seemed so counter-intuitive. She stopped interacting with him—and rightly so, because she didn't 'know' him. How could he get her to know him in a world where six-degrees-of-separation is so pre-1990s?

And how would he gather thirty thousand words now?

Sangharsh sat and thought hard for hours. Then, suddenly, it all came to him. His entire life seemed like a conspiracy designed by the universe—just to bring him to the crossroad he was standing at right now. Was all this a result of the actions he had undertaken through his life—and failed, almost always? Or was an alternate destiny created by his failed actions? Which road would Sangharsh take from here—the road he wanted to tread, or the road destiny had paved for him? Or would he unknowingly sabotage his chances, yet again?

Despite being unsure of his writing skills, Sangharsh started to write, and then e-mailed samples to the publisher. Within hours, he received a reply saying that his work was full of grammatical errors but that the Editorial Board had found the content and concept 'amazing' with 'really good potential'. They agreed to publish his work after polishing up the grammar. Sangharsh breathed a sigh of relief. He had not been misled into believing that the events that unfolded in his life were indeed 'amazing'.

He would create something that would last forever. People from around the world would read it. People living on the planet thousands of years after him would read what Sangharsh would write now. Who knows, they both might leaf through it in their 'next life'—with or without keeping the 'promise'.

Thus, despite being a fiercely private guy, Sangharsh (metaphorically) lifted his right hand, punched his chest hard, pierced it to reach for his heart, engulfed the fragile blood-soaked beating object in his fist, plucked it out, wore it on his sleeve and began writing…

1. Managing Perceptions

Calcutta, January 1995

"You have clearly not been studying. I am afraid you will not get promoted if this sort of performance is repeated in the finals. Actually, I don't see you getting promoted at all, because I know you will need some kind of a miracle to get up to speed with the syllabus, especially with your steep learning curve."

The statement, made by his class teacher, came down on Sangharsh Vashisht like a ton of bricks. The only dominant thought that occupied his mind was his reputation among the girls, which he thought he had gained favorably over the past few months, ever since he had joined the school. Sangharsh had no concerns about his career—all he thought about was how the girls would react if he failed. The ones who fancied him, would obviously not consider him anymore, and the ones he would come across would definitely not fancy someone who had flunked his exams.

Sangharsh had joined the co-educational school in class eleven after scoring poorly in the Indian Certificate of Secondary Education (ICSE) exam. He did not even manage sixty percent, and barely scored around forty percent in English. *Julius Caesar*, which was a major part of his English syllabus, couldn't rescue him, as Sangharsh could not "conquer" him. Sangharsh was clearly not a good student—he was always below average. In all the classes leading up to the tenth standard, he struggled to get promoted from one class to the next—every freakin' year.

However, miraculously, he always managed to crawl through and never failed.

The same pattern was being repeated, so he should have been used to it. However, this time round, he had something more at stake, which was not a factor earlier—"chick magnetism."

It was time for Sangharsh to think hard and strategize about how not to fail. He knew studies were not his forte, and just studying and writing the exams would not serve the purpose. He had to work on 'something else'.

For the first time in his life, he would create a strategy for something on which his life depended.

After a lot of brainstorming with himself, he came up with the following:

1. He had to study, somewhat—that could not be avoided at this point.
2. He had to portray to the teachers that he was studying. *Very hard.*

And he knew quite well that points 1 and 2 were not interlinked.

Incidentally, that was his first ever experiment with 'perception management'—it is not what you do, it is what the people who matter think about what you do.

Sangharsh became very active in class and asked a lot of questions. He prepared for the classes by reading up beforehand. He was one of the first in the class to raise his hand when the teacher asked a question, regardless of whether he knew the answer or not. Some teachers had the habit of picking on the students who did not put up their hand; when that student couldn't answer, someone who had put up her/his hand was asked to explain. He knew the answer at times—if he didn't, he managed a sneak peek at the book before being asked.

He visited the teachers' houses after school hours with questions and sought clarifications, even if he did not need them. That way, the teachers would surely know that he was preparing very hard.

While Sangharsh did study a bit, he made it seem that studying was the only thing he was doing—which was not entirely true.

Sangharsh loved two things—sleeping and playing sports. He could sleep anywhere, at any time of the day, irrespective of the surroundings—noisy or otherwise. He used to sleep so much that his mother once took him to the family doctor fearing he might be suffering from some illness. The doctor looked into Sangharsh's eyes for a few moments, turned to his mother, laughed and said, "*Sukhi aatma hai. Soney dijiye jitna sota hai.* (He is a happy soul. Let him sleep however much he wants to.)"

As for sports, though he was not good at anything in particular, he loved to play some sport or the other. He played cricket for the school and neighborhood teams and participated in badminton, tennis, table tennis, basketball, soccer, rifle shooting and any other sport he could participate in. He had to play some sport or the other every single day—it was non-negotiable. So, he had to strategize and implement his 'perception management' whenever he was not sleeping or playing any sport.

His active participation in the classroom, coupled with his visits to teachers' houses and *appearing* genuinely interested in studies seemed to have worked. Soon, the teachers began to talk about him in the staff room. A positive perception about him was built up successfully.

Sangharsh knew that, while correcting papers, if the teachers found the answers of a good student to be very lengthy, they would not go through every word but, instead, award marks based on perception. Thus, all he had to do was write lengthy answers. He was, however, mindful of the fact that there had to be some substance in them as well. However, the same substance, without the new perception, would have been viewed differently—and that difference could make all the difference. It did—he got promoted, though not with flying colors. He just 'managed'.

Now that he had passed, he walked with a swagger—with his collar pulled up and sleeves rolled, expecting to be surrounded by girls, with whom he would paint the town in all hues of red. He would pick and choose the ones he would date and the ones he would reject.

But nothing of that sort happened.

It turned out that the world Sangharsh was living in—wherein he thought he was a rock star and a 'chick magnet'—was far from reality. The girls had been just curious about him, as he was new to the school, in the same way they were curious about other newcomers. He had incorrectly assumed that he could 'read' and 'understand' girls. However, the silver lining to this misconception was pretty obvious to him after he got promoted.

Now that he knew he was not able to attract girls effortlessly, he had to do 'something else'.

But:

He didn't know how to *patao* (woo) a girl, which he never learnt.

And:

He didn't know what real love was. Yet.

2. Timing is Everything

"Wow! That is such a wonderful piece of writing! I think I would need to check your class ten results to verify how much you actually got in English," Tanaya complimented Sangharsh.

For the first time ever, someone had praised Sangharsh for his academic capabilities. He was touched. Having spent almost a year in the same class, he knew that Tanaya's compliment was genuine and she was not merely being polite. And that was the only 'reading' and 'understanding' about a girl he did correctly.

In class twelve, while making several attempts at 'something else', none of which worked, Sangharsh figured that he was somewhat relatively 'okay' at writing. He would write essays on random topics and show them to girls (never to boys)—for which he received lavish praise. This ignited an idea in his head: "Girls must be attracted to good students!" How stupid of him not to realize this earlier! This singular thought set the ball rolling for his action in the run-up to the Board exams. Now that he did not have the option of using 'perception management', since it was an external exam, this idea became his driving force. Luckily, this happened many months before the final exams, so he had ample time to work on this 'something else'.

Sangharsh made all the right moves—he attended tuitions under the right teachers, surrounded himself with good students, did group studies and studied by himself, too, but saw no major change – he just could not get better at studies. However, he still played some sport or the other—every single day.

He wanted to score good marks very badly but didn't know how. In the tests running up to the finals, he scored average and (in some cases) below-average marks. He worried that he wouldn't manage to get even sixty percent. What if he got poor grades in English? His entire efforts of brandishing essays in front of girls would go down the drain! What would Tanaya think? She might even assume that the essays he wrote were not originally his. The very thought was catastrophic!

The last set of exams before the finals were called 'rehearsals', and the marks given for those were supposed to be an indicator of the final results. Sangharsh performed very poorly. The vernacular teacher warned him, "*Sangharsh, tumhara jo hai kuch nahi ho sakta. Chalees percent mila hai Hindi mein, just pass hue ho. Board exam mein fail ho jaaoge.* (Sangharsh, you will not be able to achieve anything. You got forty percent in Hindi and just managed to pass. You will fail in the Board exam.)"

He didn't even appear for one paper, as he was not prepared. He thought it was better to be marked 'absent' than to flunk. But he couldn't do that for more than one paper—he wouldn't have been allowed to appear for the finals if he did not appear for more than one exam.

Given the score of forty percent in one paper, having been absent for one, and with just about average or below-average marks in others, Sangharsh was shitting bricks.

To make matters worse, the Board exams were scheduled bang in the middle of the 1996 Cricket World Cup. The kind of sports enthusiast that Sangharsh was, with his love for cricket in particular, he sensed trouble—major trouble. He didn't know what 'else' to do.

With nothing coming to mind, he decided to let go and not worry at all. He just knew he had to play the 'innings' of his life with whatever resources he had at that point in time. He started living by the second. He enjoyed watching the matches. He would steal some time from in between watching cricket to study—it should have been the other way around, but he did what he had to do. And he still played some sport or the other. Every. Single. Day.

Just a day before the English exam, which was the first, two things happened:

1. Sangharsh was walking back home with a bat in his hand, after playing cricket, when he bumped into Tripti, his neighbor, on the street. She asked him, surprised, "Aren't you appearing for your Board exam tomorrow? How come you are playing?" Tripti sounded as if Pakistan had attacked India and Sangharsh, as Army General, was not doing anything about it. Tripti was a few batches senior to Sangharsh. She went to a very good school and had written the same Board exam just a few years ago. She was the school topper.

Sangharsh smiled, adjusted the grip of his bat, looked up and said, "Tripti di, I am so lucky to have bumped into you at this moment! We were supposed to cross paths for a reason—the reason being that you will now give me some last-minute tips on how to ace an English exam." Tripti smiled lovingly and said, "Okay." What followed for the next half an hour was one of the most enriching sessions Sangharsh ever had—he learnt about things he had never learned at school or tuitions. He took mental note of *everything* she said. *Every little thing.*

2. The moment he reached home, the phone rang. Sangharsh was pleased to hear the voice of his close friend, Vehant. The two of them went back a long way, as classmates and best buddies from class four. Vehant always stood first or second in class. He had been the school topper in the tenth Board exams, and then moved to what was arguably the best school in the city to continue his studies until the twelfth standard. Even though Vehant was a science student and Sangharsh was in commerce, English was common to both.

Sangharsh checked the battery on the cordless phone before going to his room. Thankfully, it was fully charged—somehow, he knew it would be a long one.

"What's up, dumbass? Ready to score forty-something in English tomorrow? Just like ICSE!" Vehant laughed.

"Don't make me feel worse, dude. As it is, girls are not giving me attention. God knows what will happen if I don't do well this time. I have even stopped bothering," Sangharsh said.

"Now listen, you dumbo. Grab a pen and paper and shut yourself off from the rest of the world for as long as it takes," Vehant instructed him.

For the next two hours, Vehant imparted as much knowledge as he could, from whatever hc learnt over the past two years. Sangharsh took notes and held onto every comma and full stop that Vehant was uttering, knowing fully well that he was being given academic dope from one of the best schools of the city, if not the country.

When the conversation ended, Sangharsh heard a dying beep from the cordless phone. As he went to put it back to charge, he heard a commentary piece from an on-going cricket match: "Effortlessly flicked for a six!"

He instantly thought about:

1. The chance meeting with Tripti.
2. The two-hour telephone session with Vehant a day before an important exam.
3. The battery dying just after they said 'good luck' to each other.
4. The commentary piece he had just heard.

He smiled and said to himself, "Timing is everything."

3. Results to Remember

The exams began. Now that Sangharsh had decided to take it easy, he was nonchalant. He was surprised to see that he could easily fit in the suggestions given by both Tripti and Vehant. He smiled and reminded himself about 'timing'. While writing the exams, he secretly wished he could watch the match that was going on.

During the holidays between two exams—during one of the most important tests of his life—Sangharsh watched all the matches in which India played. Ball by ball. Both innings.

While taking the exams, Sangharsh wrote whatever 'appeared' to him at that moment. He did not bother about the results.

However, there was one thing stuck in his mind—attracting girls. Now, he knew his limitations and felt he would not be able to attract them by being a 'good student'. So, he would have to work again on 'something else'.

After a few months, it was time for results. As the days inched forward, Sangharsh couldn't help but ponder about his fate. Even though he had decided that he would not think about it, he grew more and more anxious.

On the day the results were out, Sangharsh was so nervous that he did not even go to school to check his marks. His friend Rohan called him.

"*Saale, cheating-weeting kiya tha kya? Itne numbers kahan se laya?* (Did you cheat? How did you manage to get such marks?)" Rohan exclaimed.

"*Matlab? Sixty percent mila kya kam se kam?* (What do you mean? Did I get at least sixty percent or not?)" Sangharsh murmured, biting the nail of his left index finger nervously.

"Eighty-four percent," Rohan announced.

Sangharsh did not know what hit him. He went blank for a few moments. Then, he asked in a shaky voice, "Are you sure these are my marks?"

"Yes, buddy. *Itne marks mein tow do garib students pass ho jaatey.* (Such marks are enough for two poor students to pass.)" Rohan joked.

It took Sangharsh a while to confirm that he was not dreaming. When he gathered his wits, he asked a very important question: "How much did I get in English?" He was thinking about the essays he would show the girls, especially Tanaya.

"Eighty-eight!" Rohan exclaimed.

"Whaaaaaaaaaat? That's more than double of what I got in ICSE!" Sangharsh yelled.

"And you got eighty-eight in Hindi too! You must meet our Hindi teacher soon," Rohan added enthusiastically. Sangharsh could sense his naughty smile.

Sangharsh immediately called Vehant to tell him that his session just a day before the English exam had yielded such results. He was not surprised to learn that Vehant had gotten more than ninety percent in most papers. Sangharsh then went to Tripti's house to thank her for the valuable tips.

Now that Sangharsh had scored relatively good marks, he again walked with a swagger—with his collar pulled up and sleeves rolled, expecting to be surrounded by girls with whom he would paint the town in all hues of red. He would pick and choose the ones he would date and the ones he would reject.

But nothing of that sort happened.

During his time in classes eleven and twelve, Sangharsh made some fabulous friends—many of them from his group of buddies became couples and few of them went through break-ups. Some even got back together. Sangharsh witnessed all this and expected to learn a few things.

But:

He still didn't know how to *patao* a girl, which he never learnt.

And:

He still didn't know what real love was. Yet.

4. Time For 'Something Else'

"What? Are you sure you saw it right?" Tanaya asked bewildered, disappointed and angry.

"Fortunately or unfortunately, yes. It is forty-two percent," Sangharsh replied, trying to look calm.

"What is so 'fortunate' about that?" Tanaya shrieked angrily.

"Well, I graduated!" retorted Sangharsh, projecting the 'glass-half-full' story.

"What good can these graduation marks do for you? I am sure you realize that this is as good as flunking! Most of the good B-Schools have a cut-off of fifty percent for even applying. What will you do?" Tanaya shouted, now half-angry and half-sad.

"I don't know," Sangharsh whispered.

After many years of friendship, which grew stronger over time, they got into a relationship—just a few months before the final graduation exams. The exams that would set the pace for the beginning and, subsequently, the rest of their career—in which Sangharsh got screwed, royally.

Tanaya was genuinely concerned, as she was very worried about their future together. She came from a well-educated family and her father was a highly respected senior banker. For her parents to accept him, Sangharsh had to have a decent career. He came from a business family (both paternal and maternal sides) where no one had ever held a 'job' per se.

With just forty-two percent marks in graduation, he didn't have many choices. Joining his dad's business was not an option for Sangharsh, as he was never inclined towards it.

He had to carve a career in a conventional way where students got good marks, then went for higher studies, got good marks there and then got good placements with good companies, earned a good salary and married a good girl. None of this would happen for Sangharsh as he fumbled at the first check-point.

Sangharsh needed to do 'something else'—again.

Tanaya, on the other hand, got an internship at one of the top-ranked foreign banks. That became a huge motivating factor for Sangharsh and he was desperate to land a similar job. After several failed attempts at landing some job or the other at any bank, Sangharsh managed to get a job at a Direct Sales Agency or DSA (agencies appointed by banks to sell their financial products) of a foreign bank as a sales officer for selling personal loans. Coincidentally, it was the same bank that Tanaya was interning with.

'Ah! Selling money! Who doesn't need money? It should be a cakewalk!' Sangharsh thought to himself, only to realize a few days into the job that banks only lend money to people who can prove they don't need any.

Never in his wildest dreams had he imagined that selling money could be so difficult. The people who needed money were not eligible, and the people who were eligible didn't need it—and that was not the only issue at hand.

"Can I see your visiting card, please?" The demand was made by a balding, clean-shaven, middle-aged potential customer who was sitting across a huge desk. The man was wearing a crumpled yellow shirt, with the top button undone, and a clashing red tie.

"Here it is, sir," Sangharsh had to stand and extend his arms to reach the General Manager of a Government of India undertaking, whom he had met as a result of a 'cold call'.

"Who let you inside? Did you seek appointment with my secretary?" the man questioned him, despite knowing fully well that Sangharsh had just barged in.

"I am afraid not, sir. No one was there at the secretary's desk…I found your door open and, hence, came in. I am sorry. Should I come back after getting an appointment?" Sangharsh asked.

"You said you are from a bank and you can get me money?" the man asked sarcastically.

"Sir, I sell personal loans on behalf of a bank and I can get you money if you are eligible," Sangharsh corrected him cautiously.

"But your visiting card doesn't bear any bank's name," the 'potential client' countered.

"Sir, it is a DSA. I am employed with a company that sells personal loans on behalf of the bank. If you have a requirement and are eligible, I can get you the loan. You have nothing to lose apart from photocopies of a few documents," Sangharsh reasoned with him.

"Hmm…okay. Collect the documents from my secretary and get me the money fast," the man uttered urgently.

Sangharsh was elated. That was his first sale—that too, in the first week of work. The 'sale' motivated him to work harder and get more business. He would reach office in the morning and leave immediately for 'meetings', most of which would be cold calls.

He would enter a building, take the elevator to the top floor and do cold calls across all offices on all floors while coming down the stairs. On most occasions, he was not entertained. However, he realized that every door that was shut helped him get closer to the next sale. There would be days—frequently at that—when he would skip lunch because he wanted an extra meeting. Eventually, he would have to eat something from a roadside vendor after six in the evening, before starting on a two-hour journey back to office to complete documentation and reports. More often than not, he would go home after 10pm.

Sangharsh slogged because he had been told that good performers were likely to be recruited by the bank. And he was dying to get a visiting card of a bank—it didn't matter even if the designation was that of a proverbial sweeper.

"I have some news! Guess what?" Sangharsh smiled as he asked Tanaya.

"Hmm…you got an offer to join the bank?" Tanaya said enthusiastically, hoping fervently that it was true.

"Unfortunately, no," Sangharsh said in a defeated tone. "But I got a promotion."

"Wow! That must be a first for this DSA! A promotion within a month of joining!" Tanaya was elated.

"I don't know. Maybe…" Sangharsh wondered aloud.

Not that the promotion with a DSA mattered to Sangharsh—all he wanted was to be recruited by a proper bank, so that he could call himself a banker and work on being accepted by Tanaya's parents.

"I know you are the best performer we have, tiger, but I cannot change the bank's human resources (HR) policy," Sameer reasoned. "One needs to be either a chartered accountant (CA) or a Master of Business Administration (MBA) from a tier-one B-school to be employed in a decent post." Sameer was the bank's manager who was responsible for the DSA. He was a graduate from the famed Indian Institute of Management (IIM).

"But I don't need a decent post, Sameer. Any post would do as long as it is with the bank," Sangharsh said.

"Look, you will not be doing justice to your talent if you stay behind a desk the whole day. You are mcant to do bigger things in life, tiger. You are that material. I sense one when I see one," Sameer tried to motivate Sangharsh.

Sangharsh was not sure if it was a genuine compliment or just a ploy to motivate and retain him. Whatever it was, it did not work. Sangharsh quit.

"What? You just got a promotion and you quit! Why?" Tanaya was confused.

"Because I want to prepare for the CAT exam and do an MBA from a tier-one business school. The IIMs don't have a fifty percent cut-off criteria this year," Sangharsh proclaimed.

Tanaya was very happy to hear this, but she knew that it would not be easy for Sangharsh, given his previous academic 'achievements'. However, she stood beside him like a rock and really wished he could crack it.

"I am happy that you are giving it a shot. Later in life, you will not look back and say 'I never tried'," she said wisely. Sangharsh nodded in agreement wondering about how Tanaya seemed wise beyond her years.

Sangharsh joined tutorials with some of his friends, who were excellent students. He studied hard, worked on mock-tests, and consulted seniors who had made it to the IIMs. He did whatever he could to get up to the level where he could crack the CAT exam—but, unfortunately, he couldn't. And since he had applied only to IIMs and other tier-one B-Schools, he didn't have anywhere to go.

With the option of becoming a banker going out of the window, Sangharsh needed to do 'something else', yet again.

5. The Beginning of the End

With the advent of dot.com and e-commerce, information technology or IT seemed to be booming, and one could make a decent career out of it. Sangharsh decided to jump on the bandwagon and enrolled for an IT course in software engineering. At the end of the course, he couldn't write a simple two-line program in any language to save his life.

His strategy of building an IT career fell flat. He thought, maybe, he was good for nothing.

Tanaya, on the other hand, was very good at her job and proved herself during the internship. She received glowing recommendations from her seniors and secured a good job at one of the bank's associate companies.

"Well, we are an IT start-up, and we could do with more hands in sales. If you are interested in a sales role, we could consider your job application," stated the CEO of the IT Company, whose visiting card bore the names of IIT and IIM, his alma mater.

Armed with a software engineering certificate, Sangharsh was doing the rounds of IT companies, hoping to land a decent job. However, he was turned down for two major reasons:

1. Global IT meltdown had set in; and, more importantly,
2. He did not know anything about software engineering.

Given the constraints on hand, Sangharsh considered it lucky to even have an offer. He grabbed it, hoping he would learn a great deal from an IIT-and-IIM boss and team members of similar caliber.

The environment at work was very technical for Sangharsh, and, more often than not, stuff would fly over his head. However, he managed to hold on. A few months into the job, he figured that he did not belong to the industry. He wondered if, at all, he belonged anywhere.

With each passing day, Sangharsh grew more and more insecure about his career and his future with Tanaya. He began to think about why Tanaya would want to stay on with such a failure. He grew extremely restless and began to suspect that Tanaya was losing interest in him. As a result, he became very possessive about her.

"Why are you wearing that dress? Don't you have something decent to wear?" Sangharsh snapped at Tanaya when he saw her in a sleeveless dress.

"What's wrong with you? Even my parents do not object to my dressing sense," Tanaya argued.

"Your parents don't approve of me. Will you listen to them on this count, too?" Sangharsh countered.

"The way you are behaving of late, I think I should," Tanaya warned him.

That sentence was like the beginning of the end for Sangharsh. He got scared—very scared—of losing her.

Every guy in the world seemed like a potential threat to Sangharsh. He grew suspicious that Tanaya would get attracted to someone else and leave him. He felt helpless.

"I have been trying to call you for so long. Your number was constantly busy. Who were you speaking to?" Sangharsh questioned Tanaya.

"I was speaking to a colleague," Tanaya said curtly.

"Why do you need to speak with a colleague on a Sunday? And for so long?" Sangharsh shouted.

"Don't shout at me! It's none of your business whom I speak to and for how long!" Tanaya screamed at him.

Sangharsh put the phone down without saying a word. Tanaya didn't call back.

Sangharsh felt miserable. He only thought about how he felt. He did not think about what Tanaya was going through because of him.

The next day, Tanaya called Sangharsh and said, "We need to talk. When can we meet?"

Sangharsh had learned enough by then to understand that, when a woman said she needed to 'talk', it meant trouble.

They met later in the day.

"Look, Sangharsh, I don't think we should continue this relationship any longer," Tanaya said in a matter-of-fact tone but tears rolled down her cheeks.

"But why?" Sangharsh barely managed to whisper, as the ground beneath his feet seemed to move. "Is there someone else?" His eyes were moist, swollen and red.

"No." Tanaya wiped her tears, and then shed some more.

"Is that you, or someone else speaking?" Sangharsh asked, looking straight into her tearful eyes.

Tanaya broke the eye-lock, looked down and said, "Doesn't matter. Promise me that you will take care of yourself."

Sangharsh was neither listening properly nor thinking straight. His senses were clouded. He kept on saying, "I don't know", then turned and walked away.

Sangharsh was alone. Tanaya felt sorry for him.

Since Tanaya and Sangharsh were from the same school and the same batch, they had several mutual friends. After the break-up,

Sangharsh started to get calls from friends asking him to meet up, play and party, but he was too heart-broken to think about anything. He went into a shell.

He walked like a living corpse, oblivious to the passage of time. He took leave from work, cut himself off socially and even stopped playing sports. He had no sense of hunger or thirst. Every day, he would go to a park and sit on a bench for hours and stare into space.

Tanaya was as heart-broken as Sangharsh, if not more, but Sangharsh only thought about his suffering. The fact that his immaturity was the main reason Tanaya had broken their relationship did not occur to him. He waited endlessly for Tanaya's call.

Sangharsh had to join work after a few days, as couldn't be on leave perpetually. He didn't anticipate what awaited him on his return.

Sangharsh's boss called him into his office and said, "Sangharsh, you have been useful for the company and I thank you for your contribution. However, unfortunately, there is some bad news, which I did not want to share while you were on leave. The global IT meltdown is affecting our company, and we need to close shop immediately. Please look for an alternative. I know a few companies who are recruiting, but they need…"

Sangharsh cut him off in mid-sentence: "I know. They need engineers, MBAs or post-graduates and I do not fit in. It's okay, boss. I understand, and I truly appreciate your support. How many days do I have?"

"Today will be your last working day, Sangharsh," his boss said sympathetically.

Lightning had struck twice in a few days. This was as bad as it could get. He lost his job. His girlfriend broke up with him.

Sangharsh was completely down and out. In the darkest hour of his life, he reminded himself of what Tanaya had once said: "Remember, it is always darkest before dawn." Sangharsh hoped to see the light of dawn somewhere and again wondered at Tanaya's wisdom. She had taught him so much about life that he would forever remain grateful to her. He rued the fact that he was not a part of her life anymore.

6. Kafkaesque

After a few months, even though Sangharsh was still nursing his wounds, he slowly started hunting for a job; he met friends and even started playing some sports. Life was edging towards normalcy again. He sensed that many women were attracted to him. On average, one out of every two women he met was drawn to him; at times the ratio even reached 1:1. He couldn't understand why, but he was not bothered. He found it ironical—at one point in his life, he was dying to get attention from girls; now, when he was getting lots of attention, he didn't want any. He kept thinking about Tanaya and hoped she would get back with him soon.

One day, Ram, one of Sangharsh's former colleagues from the IT Company called him. "Dude, are you still looking for a job?" he enquired.

"Yes, I am, but you are probably aware that I am not an engineer, CA, MBA or post-graduate. I am just a plain graduate with pathetic marks." Sangharsh was clearly frustrated.

"I know, man. But this is a job with an Indian private bank and their minimum requirement is just a degree in any stream," Ram said enthusiastically.

"What? Are you serious? Bank?" Sangharsh's mind raced back in no time; he still craved a bank's visiting card. "Will my visiting card bear the bank's name?" he asked.

"No, this is not on the bank's payroll. However, this company is the sales arm of the bank—not a DSA. So, you will have opportunities to perform and get recruited on the bank's pay roll. It has happened before," Ram assured Sangharsh.

"I will take it," Sangharsh declared.

"My friend, you have to appear for an interview first and get selected. Then, you can say what you just said," Ram brought Sangharsh back to the ground reality.

Sangharsh went for the interview. A few questions later, he was selected. The role involved selling corporate accounts—since Sangharsh had experience in selling banking products, it was not difficult for him to crack the interview.

He was asked to join immediately.

On the way to the office for his first day of work, Sangharsh texted Tanaya: 'On my way to start a new life with a new job; wish me luck.' He got no reply—that hurt real bad.

"Okay guys, this is your first working day. Let me set some rules straight," Tony was addressing the newcomers. Tony was Assistant Vice President of the bank and was in charge of the corporate accounts team. He had joined the bank just a few days before Sangharsh.

"As your boss, I am entitled to know what you are doing, where you are going, whom you are meeting and how you are closing the sale," Tony continued.

Sangharsh thought, 'What, where, whom and how—all this in one sentence on the first day is not a good sign.'

He was right. Tony was a micro-manager and a very intrusive boss; he wanted to know everything about everybody. He had a few favorites, who would get away with even murder, and there were others who were not in his 'good books'. Sangharsh topped the second list.

Tony picked on Sangharsh for the smallest of reasons. Sangharsh had to fill in the daily sales report every day, without fail, while some others had the luxury of filling it once a week. Tony also interrogated Sangharsh on every detail of the report—the interrogation was akin to that of an FBI agent interrogating a serial killer.

Since Sangharsh met his sales targets, there wasn't much Tony could do. However, Sangharsh felt cornered and realized that Tony would never recommend his name for direct bank employment. This was made worse by the fact that the immediate boss's recommendation was a primary requirement. Sangharsh was forced to look for a job elsewhere. He again targeted banks. He sent his resume to placement consultants who specialized in financial sector recruitments, and even applied directly to a few banks. He did not get a positive response from anywhere. He was stuck with Tony.

One day, while walking back to office after a long day of multiple meetings, Sangharsh bumped into one of his friends. They chatted for a bit, and then she suggested that they have tender coconut water from a roadside vendor. The entire episode did not last more than fifteen minutes.

The next morning, during the team meeting, Tony pulled out a blank sheet of paper and extended it towards Sangharsh as he announced sarcastically, "A little bird whispered in my ears that 'someone' will resign today because that 'someone' was busy having coconut water with his girlfriend during office hours."

Sangharsh wasn't sure if Tony had seen them or if it had been someone from his 'good books'. He was not bothered—this episode had crossed all possible limits. If nothing drastic was done instantly, he would be jobless again for no fault of his or the economy's. His mind raced in search of a plausible solution. Every second lost was taking him closer to being without a job. And then, he had a 'light bulb' moment. Before Tony could reach him, Sangharsh reached out, snatched the paper from Tony's hand and rushed out of the meeting. He went straight to the office of the Regional Head, who was Tony's boss.

Sangharsh spent almost half an hour in the office. Before the meeting ended, the Regional Head said, "Don't worry. Please ask Tony to see me immediately." Sangharsh smiled and left. The smile turned into a smirk the moment he left the office.

Sangharsh strode over to Tony, signaled to the left with raised eyebrows and announced, "He is calling you."

Tony did not see this coming and did not know how to react in front of the team. All he could manage was, "Okay, I will see him after the meeting."

"He is calling you now," Sangharsh insisted with a sense of urgency in his voice.

Before Tony could respond, he received a call on his phone. The entire team heard him say, "Yes, boss, coming right now," he said and rushed out.

Tony emerged from the Regional Head's office after an hour, and immediately addressed the team in a way that seemed like a transformation from a caterpillar to a butterfly.

"From now on, if anyone needs any assistance from me, please do not think twice before asking. I am here to help you achieve your goals and I will ensure that we work as a cohesive unit. And I do not want any attrition in the team," Tony announced.

Everyone looked at each other and then collectively looked at Sangharsh, who couldn't hide his smirk.

After the meeting, Tony went over to Sangharsh and said, "I want to accompany you for some of your meetings."

Sangharsh responded with a smile, "Sure."

After some time, Sangharsh overheard Tony say to someone over the phone, "Yes, I will send my resume across today itself."

That was the first time he realized that he could pray sincerely for someone he did not get along with. Sangharsh had prayed that

Tony should land a job elsewhere and move out of the company and his life.

Sangharsh reached home that night, only to realize that his cell phone was missing. He frantically called his number—it kept ringing for some time, then it was switched off. He realized that his pocket had been picked.

He sighed, "What an eventful day!"

7. Money Can Buy Happiness

Sangharsh had a meeting scheduled for the next day at a distant place, and he had to travel by train. Since Tony had asked to accompany him for meetings, Sangharsh called him along. Tony was a bit reluctant due to the long distance, but was reminded of the conversation he had had with his boss and agreed to go. However, he said he would travel separately and that they would meet directly at the specified place. Sangharsh happily thought, 'Good—at least I get to travel peacefully.'

At the railway station, while Sangharsh was marching towards the platform to catch the train, a girl and a boy approached him, seeking alms—they seemed to be around five to seven years old. Sangharsh usually never gave money to beggars, as there was no way to figure out how it would be used. However, he adored children and always had a soft spot for them. He asked the kids to accompany him to the nearest vendor and bought them cakes and a cola each. He unwrapped the cake and handed them their 'gift'. The moment the children laid their hands on the food, they looked at Sangharsh lovingly and smiled so warmly, with a twinkle in their eyes, that he was touched. His heart seemed to expand with happiness. It was a very fulfilling experience. Since he had to catch a train, he walked towards the platform but kept looking back at them. When he saw their faces filled with love and contentment, his happiness grew. He kept looking at them till they faded into the distance. He thought, 'Whoever says money can't buy happiness should try something similar to what I just did.'

Sangharsh reached and saw Tony waiting for him at the destination. Sangharsh was worried that Tony would be upset for making him wait, but Tony just smiled and greeted him. Sangharsh wondered if that was the effect of the closed-door discussion Tony had had with his boss.

They met the Vice President–Finance of a large corporate. About ten minutes into the meeting, Tony's cell phone rang. He excused himself, saying he needed to take the 'urgent' call. Sangharsh continued with the discussion. Within a minute, Tony came back, extended his cell phone towards Sangharsh and said, "It's for you."

Sangharsh was perplexed. He took the phone and excused himself.

"I am sorry. I had to call your boss because your cell phone was unreachable," a lady stated apologetically.

"Ah…Yes, I am afraid I lost my phone yesterday," Sangharsh said while trying to figure out her identity. He removed the phone from his ear for a split second and looked at the screen for the caller's name. It read, 'Ms. Jassi'.

Sangharsh remembered that he had sent her his resume a few days back. He deduced that:

1. She was one of the most influential placement consultants in the finance industry.
2. She specialized in placements with foreign banks.
3. Tony had placed his resume with her—why else would her number be stored on his phone?
4. She apparently knew Tony was his boss.

"There is a written test on English and mathematics today at 6pm at Ethal Bank. Please meet the HR manager, take my reference and be on time. And carry a calculator along for mathematics portion of the test," Ms. Jassi announced, assuming that Sangharsh knew who she was and that he would follow every word of what she was saying.

Without even asking about the role, package or designation, Sangharsh said gratefully, "Yes, sure. Thank you, Ms. Jassi," and hung up. He was happy and terrified at the same time for the following reasons:

1. Ethal Bank was highly respected worldwide. While dreaming of being employed by a good bank, he had never even considered Ethal as he thought he could never get a job there, given his academic background. Now, he had an opportunity that was beyond his dreams.
2. His tenth grade English marks and graduation exam marks haunted him.
3. If he got in, Sangharsh could finally get a bank's visiting card—that too, from one of the best in the world!
4. Would Tony let him go for the test within 'office hours'?

Sangharsh went back inside the room, handed the phone to Tony with a grateful smile and resumed the meeting, hoping it would end soon. Thankfully, it did.

After the meeting ended, Tony turned to Sangharsh and asked, "How come I do not receive calls for opportunities with such organizations?" Sangharsh figured that Ms. Jassi had briefed Tony about the reason for her call.

Sangharsh wanted to say, "Well, you did receive the call, except that it wasn't meant for you." He wisely refrained from making such a comment and instead said, "Tony, I need to be there at six for a written test."

Tony thought for a while and said, "Okay. However, please conclude the second meeting you have, and then go wherever you need to."

"Tony, that meeting is in the opposite direction of where I need to go. If I go there, I will be delayed for the test. I will reschedule that meeting for tomorrow," Sangharsh said in a wounded tone.

Tony did some calculations in his head and then threw a bomb: "No. You need to go for that meeting today."

Sangharsh looked at his watch, did some 'speed = distance/time' calculation in his head and said, "Okay. I will."

"I will cross-check with the client in the evening," Tony threatened him.

Tony did not know Sangharsh. If he had to disregard Tony's instructions, he would have pulled out a sheet of paper, written his resignation and then left. However, Sangharsh did not bother as he was already racing against time. He just nodded and set off.

He rushed to the station, took the train and reached the city. While walking out of the platform, he looked around, hoping to catch a glimpse of the children he had seen earlier. He couldn't find them; he prayed for their wellbeing and ran towards the taxi stand.

"Salt Lake," Sangharsh barked as he opened the door of a cab and got in.

"*Jaabo na.* (I will not go.)" the pot-bellied cab driver, who was wearing a torn vest, said in a nonchalant tone.

Sangharsh was born and raised in Calcutta and, hence, was aware of the antics of cabbies. While rushing towards the taxi stand, he had factored probable situations and thought of the sequence of events that might play out—with multiple possible solutions.

"*Jaabo na mane? Ekhkhuni Police ke daakbo. 'No refusal' er case diye debe.* (What do you mean by 'I will not go'? I will call the cops right now. You will be booked under 'no refusal' case.)" Sangharsh tried to scare him.

"*Ja khushi korun. Jaabo na maane jaabo na.* (Do whatever you wish. I will not go.)" the cabbie retorted. Any further argument would have been a waste of time and Sangharsh couldn't afford that. Getting off and attempting to take another cab would be a further waste of time.

"*Extra niye neben.* (Take extra money.)" Sangharsh offered.

The cabbie sensed his urgency and said, "*Ponchaas taka extra laagbe.* (I will take fifty bucks extra.)"

Sangharsh instantly said, "Okay." Even if the cabbie had asked for more than fifty bucks, he would have agreed.

The cab set off. Going by the speed at which it was moving, Sangharsh realized he would not finish the meeting and then reach Ethal Bank on time. He added a sweetener to the deal: "*Aapni jodi amake tirish minute ey pouchey deben tow ek sho taka extra debo.* (If you get me there within thirty minutes, I will give you a hundred bucks extra.)"

The moment Sangharsh mentioned the offer, the cabbie's spine straightened, the arms on the wheels went from the twenty-past-seven-o-clock position to a ten-past-ten-o-clock and a slight 'thud' was heard almost instantly—the sound of the accelerator hitting the floor of the car.

They reached in twenty-two minutes. "*Dada, aath minute aage pouchey diyechi, aaro kudi ta taka extra diye deben.* (I got you here eight minutes earlier, give me twenty bucks extra.)" the cabbie tried his luck.

Sangharsh was hardly listening; he had already counted out the notes when the destination was in view. He handed over the money and rushed out of the cab. He did not hear any voice coming from behind, so he assumed he must have paid the amount they agreed upon or maybe a little extra.

While 'Michael Schumacher' had been busy taking the shortest possible route to reach the destination in the quickest possible time, Sangharsh had been thinking about how he would start, conduct and conclude the meeting so that everything was covered expeditiously. His 'homework' paid off. The meeting got over and Sangharsh rushed out, hoping to find 'Schumacher' there. Unfortunately, he was gone.

"What an idiot I am! I should have retained Schumacher," Sangharsh scolded himself.

He looked for another cab frantically, but none was around. Every second lost was negatively skewing his on-time arrival at Ethal Bank.

He spotted a public bus going in the direction of his desired destination and jumped on it, thinking that it was his best bet. He rued the fact that he couldn't make any offers to the bus driver to go faster. Suddenly, it struck him that he needed to get a calculator as well—another few valuable minutes lost. Then Sangharsh looked at his watch, closed his eyes, calmed himself down and imagined stepping inside Ethal Bank at 5:58pm.

Little did he know that he was attempting to put into action a part of reality that science had not caught up with, yet. Something close to what Einstein had expounded around ninety years back—a theory called 'bending' of space and time. In 2004, NASA deployed a $700-million project called Gravity Probe B to ascertain this theory, the early results of which confirmed to a precision of better than one percent that Earth does indeed distort the fabric of space and time (Source: *The Guardian*, April 15, 2007).

The moment he imagined the arrival time, he felt a slight push—that was the effect of the bus accelerating. Miraculously, the traffic signals were all green and he reached the destination before he had hoped to. He got off and found a roadside shop that sold calculators right in front of him; he bought one and headed towards Ethal Bank. As he entered the lobby, he noticed a large wall clock—the hour hand was pointing at six, and the angle it made with the minute hand going clockwise was still an obtuse one.

"Ah! You must be Sangharsh," the HR officer greeted him cheerfully. "We were expecting you." She gestured towards the chair across her desk. Sangharsh sat down nervously and opened his bag to take out the relevant papers. He wondered if he was the only one to be called for the test—if not, why was he being addressed by name?

"We have your papers from Ms. Jassi. First, let us get on with the written test. Then, we will chat," she said in a friendly tone. Sangharsh's biggest fear was about his academic record, and he suspected that the 'chat' might have something to do with that.

He was led to the adjacent room, which was set up like a classroom. Some people were already seated; there was just one desk and chair that was unoccupied. There were eleven other candidates; since he was the last one to arrive, he had been addressed by name. He glanced around the room and was intimidated by the candidates' disposition. He was clearly the youngest—in terms of age and experience.

The test comprised of multiple-choice questions on English and mathematics. Sangharsh's CAT preparations came in handy—the pattern was similar, and this test was relatively easier. After he finished the exam, Sangharsh headed for the 'chat'.

"So Sangharsh, how was the test?" the lady asked him cheerfully.

"It was okay," Sangharsh said, anticipating the dreaded question.

"Well, I have already had this discussion with other candidates. I wanted to tell you that we have only one vacancy at the moment. The selection process involves a written test, which you just completed. If you are shortlisted, you will be called for a group discussion, followed by a personal interview. If you are selected, and should you choose to accept our offer, employment will be under a one-year contract that will be renewed based on your performance. Any questions?" The HR officer expected to hear the usual questions on compensation package, perks, benefits and so on.

Sangharsh had only one question: "If I am selected, will I get a visiting card bearing the bank's name?"

The lady laughed and responded, "Of course, you will."

Sangharsh thanked her and left. While leaving the building, he dismissed his chances of getting selected based on the 'competition' he had seen. However, he thought, 'If I get a job here, Tanaya might come back.'

The next morning, just as Sangharsh was about to leave for work, he received a call on the landline. "Hi Sangharsh, I couldn't get through to your cell phone, so I called your residence," a familiar voice said. Sangharsh instantly identified the HR lady from Ethal Bank. She continued, "Congratulations! You have been shortlisted. Please come for the group discussion and personal interview at 5pm today."

Sangharsh wasn't too excited. The written test was no big deal as the questions were relatively easy. He was expecting all twelve candidates to turn for the group discussion and interview.

He reached office and informed Tony about being shortlisted. Miraculously, Tony congratulated him and wished him all the best. He even offered to let him take the day off just in case he wanted to prepare in advance. Sangharsh couldn't believe his change of heart. He didn't take the day off as he had a few meetings planned during the day.

After conducting the meetings, Sangharsh reached Ethal Bank about half an hour before the scheduled time. He was led into a room where five candidates were seated around a large table. 'So I am not the only one who is early,' he thought. Then, he realized that the brand value of Ethal Bank was so high that no one would want to miss the opportunity. He learnt that he had been the last one to arrive and that only six candidates had been shortlisted.

Since there was some time left, the other candidates in the room started to chat about their qualifications and experience. Sangharsh felt left out. He was clearly the youngest, the most under-qualified and with the least experience. He was absolutely certain that there was no way he would be selected. He even considered walking out of that room. Then, he thought he had nothing to lose and stayed on. He was so certain that this was not meant for him that his nervousness vanished.

There was a knock at the door. A middle-aged person wearing the bank's uniform looked inside and announced, "Sangharsh Vashisht." Sangharsh put up his hand, unsure of what was in store. "Please come with me," the man said.

Sangharsh was led to another room, inside which was a panel of senior people seated behind a large desk. Sangharsh was greeted with warm smiles and asked to occupy the sole chair on the other side of the desk. Sangharsh returned their smiles with a warmer smile. He had already dismissed his chances of getting selected and was at ease.

What followed for the next half an hour was an extended chat. He was told that the group discussion has been scrapped due to time constraints; he was also informed that the sole vacancy was for the position of 'sales officer' for acquiring current accounts of businesses. He was asked about his current work profile and his interests in driving, sports, travelling, movies and so on. No tough questions. No grilling. No mention of academic (mis)achievements.

The interview ended. Sangharsh left, wondering if they had been nice to him because they had rejected him but did not unnecessarily want to seem rude.

He thought of the experience as a passing dream.

Sangharsh went about his usual business not expecting anything from the Ethal Bank interview. After three days, he received a call on his new cell phone. The lady's voice on the other end was as excited as Sangharsh ought to have been: "Congratulations! You have been selected!" Even though Sangharsh recognized the voice, he could not believe what he had heard. To be absolutely sure, he asked, "Who is this?"

"I am calling from Ethal Bank. Please come over today to have a look at the offer. Should you choose to accept it, you will need to clear certain formalities like medical tests."

"Okay, thanks. I will," Sangharsh said softly. The feeling of ecstasy was so high that it dwarfed his voice.

He immediately called Tanaya. "Guess what?"

"What?" Tanaya replied, sounding busy; she was at work.

"I got a job at Ethal Bank!" Sangharsh shouted as his ecstasy and reality met.

"Wow! Congratulations! I am very happy for you!" Tanaya sounded genuinely happy. Sangharsh saw a ray of hope.

"I am going over to complete the formalities right now. They will give me some papers, which I am sure I will not be able to understand properly. Since you come from a banking family and you have banking experience, can you help me decipher the documents, please?" he asked expectantly.

"Okay, I will. Let's meet in the evening," Tanaya responded.

Sangharsh was over the moon. Perhaps this was the light of dawn he was expecting to see for so long. He went to Ethal Bank, accepted the offer, took the documents and waited for evening.

"So, what do you think?" Sangharsh asked as Tanaya sifted through the documents. The steam from the cups of coffee formed a cloud between them.

"The papers look good. Only thing is that the employment is on contract—so, they can ask you to leave any time," she said.

"So, what do you think?" Sangharsh repeated slowly, his eyebrows raised.

Tanaya continued, still looking at the papers, "It is good but you must…" She looked up and stopped when she noticed Sangharsh's expression.

"Sangharsh, no," she said sternly.

Sangharsh took the hint—he realized that he was still not mature enough to get back with her. He didn't insist. Sangharsh went back to being normal and continued their discussion. They spoke as the cloud cleared.

8. Nova Initia

First day of work at Ethal Bank

When Sangharsh walked in to the office, Anuradha, his boss, a lady with a very pleasant and calm disposition, who had been with the bank for about ten years, greeted him and showed him his place of work. The desk had a new folder, a bunch of product documents and a box of visiting cards. Sangharsh's vision was fixated on the box. He slowly opened it and was mesmerized when he saw his name and designation alongside the bank's logo. His 'spell' was broken when he was requested by Anuradha to sit with her for a briefing session.

"We have six branches in East India—all of them are in Calcutta, and there is one sales officer attached to each branch. While most of your business should be routed to the branch you are attached to, you are free to choose the ones you want to give business to. You will be directly reporting to me, just like officers of other branches," she explained.

Then, she began to illustrate the bank's hierarchy:

"The rungs of the ladder are:

Assistant

Officer

Assistant Manager

Deputy Manager

Manager

Senior Manager

Associate Vice President

Vice President…"

Sangharsh cut her short and asked, "I am sorry for interrupting, but what are the academic qualifications required for reaching these levels?"

"Well, we do not have a set or official academic qualification requirement. However, just to give you an idea, we hire from IIMs and other tier-one business schools such as XLRI or FMS at the AVP levels," Anuradha clarified.

"Does that mean a non-MBA or just a plain graduate can also reach these positions?" Sangharsh enquired expectantly.

Anuradha thought for a while and then cautiously answered, "Technically, yes."

Sangharsh wanted to ask if someone who scored forty-two percent in his graduation exam stood a chance of progressing to these levels. He wisely chose to keep his mouth shut.

The office was spread over a vast area with an open seating system. Sangharsh pointed to a grey-haired gentleman, who was wearing a crisp white shirt with a maroon tie, and asked, "What is his designation?" He assumed that the man would be, at least, a Vice President.

"He is a manager," Anuradha said.

"Oh! And for how long has he been with the bank?" Sangharsh asked curiously.

"For about twenty years." Anuradha said. Then, understanding Sangharsh's underlying concern, she added, "Yes, and he must be around fifty years old. But look there…" She pointed towards a young man. "He is not even thirty and he is an AVP."

"Is he just a graduate?" Sangharsh enquired.

"He is from IIM–Ahmedabad." Anuradha said hesitantly and looked around to show Sangharsh something from his viewpoint.

She couldn't find any. Sangharsh understood and thought, 'Still technically possible'

"Let's talk business now," Anuradha said to divert Sangharsh's attention.

"Oh yes! That's why we are here for," Sangharsh quipped.

Anuradha smiled and took out a brochure from her drawer. "This is a new premium product we have launched across India this week and the management wants the entire sales team to focus on this," she explained.

Sangharsh took a detailed look at the brochure, and started to think about all the companies he could pitch the product to. He made a few phone calls immediately and fixed an appointment.

"Can you accompany me for the meeting I have fixed for this new product?" Sangharsh requested Anuradha.

"Absolutely. This is your first day and I don't expect you to know everything. I will be there to handhold you. Don't worry," Anuradha assured him.

Sangharsh's mind raced back to Tony, and he couldn't help thinking, 'What a contrast!'

They set out for the meeting.

Sangharsh keenly observed Anuradha as she conducted the meeting and secured the business. While leaving, Anuradha told Sangharsh enthusiastically, "You have no idea what you have done today!"

"What?" Sangharsh smiled.

"You will soon know," Anuradha responded with a broader smile.

Back at the office. Anuradha sat at her desk and began tapping on the keyboard. Sangharsh was impatient to find out what he had 'done'.

Within a minute after she finished typing, Anuradha got a call on her cell phone.

She stood up and answered, "Yes, sir! Thank you, sir! He is right here with me. Sure." Anuradha pulled the phone away from her ear, covered the microphone with her palm and whispered to Sangharsh, "Country Head from Mumbai. He wants to speak to you."

Before Sangharsh could process what was happening, Anuradha thrust the phone into his hand. A very authoritative voice spoke from the other end, "Well done, champ! Congratulations! Such an achievement on your first day with us is remarkable. Wish you all the best."

Sangharsh did not know how to respond. He just managed to say "Thank you, sir!"

He then turned to Anuradha and said in astonishment, "What was that all about?"

Anuradha mentioned that she had just sent an email to every Regional Head in the country and to the Country Head, stating that Sangharsh has gotten the first ever deal for the new product in the entire country—that too, on his first day of joining.

"But that is not true! You secured the deal. I was just watching you and learning how to conduct such meetings. It is you who did this, not me. Giving me credit for something I have not done is not fair!" Sangharsh almost fought with her.

"Relax, Sangharsh. A manager is as good as her/his team members," Anuradha smiled and winked.

That was the first lesson in leadership for Sangharsh.

After a few minutes, Anuradha looked at her computer and exclaimed, "Ah! I was kind of expecting this!"

"What now?" Sangharsh asked.

"The Country Head has just replied to my email. He has sanctioned a handsome budget for a cocktail party tomorrow evening. Our entire team, along with all branch managers, East India Head, other business heads and seniors will be present. He is terming this a 'success party'," Anuradha replied.

Sangharsh was not used to the culture. He was confused. Anuradha sensed it and said, "Welcome to the world of corporate banking."

At the cocktail party, Anuradha introduced Sangharsh to all the branch managers and other seniors as "the guy who cracked premium new business on first day". Sangharsh was embarrassed as he felt he did not deserve the attention.

"Where is your glass, rock star?" a senior asked Sangharsh.

"Sir, I don't drink," Sangharsh responded.

"What? *To kya zindagi chai aur sutta pe chalti hai*? (Do you live on tea and cigarettes then?)," he exclaimed.

Sangharsh smiled and said, "Sir, I don't smoke and I don't drink tea as well."

"What? You don't drink. You don't smoke. How will you climb the corporate ladder, my friend?" he was clearly surprised.

"I don't know, sir. Maybe I will not be able to," Sangharsh smiled.

"You should be a brand ambassador for our insurance products!" he joked as he sipped on his single malt and excused himself.

Anuradha came by and said, "All the branch managers are pulling me aside and requesting me to put you in their branch. They are fighting over you."

"But, Anuradha, how can just one deal spin off such chain of events? I mean, I have just joined. No one knows if I am consistent or not. This could be just a flash in the pan. And you did everything. I don't think this is going the right way," Sangharsh argued.

Anuradha said, "Look, we are in the business of banking, and we believe in *banking* on our people. Whatever is happening is for business, in some way or the other."

Sangharsh was even more puzzled. He was unable to fathom what Anuradha was meaning. She sensed his confusion and continued, "This entire event is serving the following business purposes:

1. You will get motivated and try and do more business to keep up your reputation.
2. Other team members will get motivated on seeing such a response for your success, so they will try to get more business. This should answer your question of why I am not taking credit. If I did, no team member would want to perform well.
3. The branch managers who are fighting over you will help you whenever you need anything, because you can technically give business to any branch. Since you have come up in the eyes of seniors here and in Mumbai, they would want to pamper you.
4. You get introduced to the right people in a 'loosened up' environment. That helps in breaking the ice and generating good work relations.

So, everything boils down to business. Nothing is an expense. Everything is an investment. It is a win-win situation."

"Phew! That's an overdose of learning for me!" Sangharsh remarked.

Soon, Sangharsh became friendly with a lot of 'right' people and also with the ones he didn't have anything to do with. He developed good relationships with everyone by solving issues, referring business, suggesting strategies to senior management—some of which were recognized and implemented—he even got awards for his business development ideas. While interacting with people he would pepper his conversations with trivia every now and then. Even though he was not a quizzard, he liked collecting and retaining interesting bits of information.

Sangharsh came across many wonderful women, too. He could sense that the 'strike rate' of women getting attracted to him was as good as before. He went out with a select few for movies, meals and drives and made some fabulous friends for lifetime. There were some girls whose intention of getting into a relationship with Sangharsh was as apparent as daylight, but Sangharsh did not reciprocate because:

He was still not completely over Tanaya and fancied his chances of getting back.

And…

He still didn't know what real love was. Yet.

9. Winning with Bollywood Moves

Sangharsh managed to secure a spot in the bank's official cricket team to play inter-corporate matches and tournaments. He never scored a century, and never played any 'match winning' innings. He was just about average—enough to secure a place in the team, and was dropped on some occasions, too.

During an inter-corporate tournament, since most senior members of the cricket team did not have enough time to play, Sangharsh was asked to captain and lead a team of boys, many of whom had recently joined various departments. It was a huge responsibility for Sangharsh, as he had never captained a team for such a serious tournament before. It was even more challenging as he did not know the strengths and weaknesses of his team members. He called the team for a practice session to observe them. Due to time constraints, he could hold only one such session.

The tournament started and the first match was played against the country's steel giant. The team had some players who had played state-level cricket, and were believed to have been mentored by players who represented India. For that match, Sangharsh listened to every team member's strategies, but none of them worked. Sangharsh's team was hit all over the park and they were bowled out miserably. Even though that loss was inevitable, it hurt Sangharsh—badly.

After the match, he didn't say anything to anyone; he sulked all evening. He thought hard about the way forward. He keenly watched the other matches, especially of teams they were likely to encounter. He went on days when his team did not have a match, just to observe their likely opponents.

The tournament had three levels—Gold, Silver and Bronze Plates. The team that lost the first match went to the Silver Plate and the team that lost two matches competed for the Bronze Plate. Sangharsh's team went to the second level—to win the Silver Plate of the tournament, they had to win every match thereafter.

Throughout the tournament, Sangharsh thought about ways to maximize his team's performance. Before going to bed, his last thought was about winning strategies; upon waking up, his first thought was the same. During matches, he listened to the suggestions from his team members, but only implemented the ones he had thought out himself. As the tournament progressed, he got to know the strengths of his team members and used suitable players for batting, bowling and field positions. The team started to win matches and reached the finals.

As expected, they faced a tough opponent in the final match. It was Team B of the same steel giant.

Sangharsh lost the toss and was asked to field first. The opponent's opening batsman, who would face the first delivery, was their best—as Sangharsh had noticed during his 'homework'. Sangharsh knew that if they could get rid of him early, they had a good chance of winning the tournament.

Sangharsh worked out a strategy to get him. He gave the ball to Samiran Ratan Kundu, the fastest bowler in his team and took the fielding position at mid-off, so that he could chat with Samiran prior to every delivery.

Before the match started, Sangharsh could sense Samiran's nervousness, which gave the batsman an advantage even before the first delivery. Sangharsh communicated the strategy to Samiran in a different way.

Sangharsh asked him, "*Amitabh Bachchan ki* Don *dekhi hai?* (Have you seen Amitabh Bachchan's *Don?*)"

Samiran was taken aback. He said, confused, "*Haan dekhi hai.* (Yes, I have watched it.)"

"*Dialogue yaad hai? 'Yeh tum jaante ho ki yeh revolver khali hai, yeh main jaanta hoon ki ye revolver khali hai. Police nahi jaanti ki yeh revolver khali hai.'* (Do you remember this dialogue: 'You know the revolver isn't loaded. I know the revolver isn't loaded. Cops don't know the revolver isn't loaded.')"

"*Haan yaad hai.* (Yes, I remember.)" Samiran responded, still not understanding where this was going.

"*Yeh tum jaante ho ki tumhari bowling ki pace kya hai, yeh mai jaanta hoon ki tumhari bowling ki pace kya hai. Lekin wo nahi jaanta ki tumhari bowling ki pace kya hai.* (You know the pace of your bowling. I know the pace of your bowling. He doesn't know the pace of your bowling.)" Sangharsh explained the strategy.

"*Haan, tow?* (So what?)" Samiran asked, fearing that Sangharsh would want him to bowl slow. That's the thing about fast bowlers—asking them to bowl slow meant the end of the world for them. Like asking a Formula 1 driver to maintain city speed limits on the racing track.

"Look, buddy, your first delivery should be pitched up—no swing, a half-volley just outside off-stump, at less than half of your original pace. And I don't want you to bowl the slower delivery from the back of your hand. It should appear like your natural pace," Sangharsh instructed him.

Samiran was visibly upset, but he nodded reluctantly. He took the run-up and bowled exactly the way Sangharsh had instructed and was hit right back over his head for a six.

Sangharsh said to himself, "Yes! This is exactly what I wanted."

The opponent team's members, who were standing outside the boundary shouted: "Great shot! *Maal bowler hai. Kha le kha le.* (He is a poor bowler. Eat him, eat him.)"

While walking back to deliver the next ball, Samiran looked at Sangharsh, raised his eyebrows and shook his head vigorously. Sangharsh patted his back, told him to relax and bowl the next delivery in exactly the same way.

Samiran was furious. First, you ask a fast bowler to bowl at less than half his pace—as a result of which he gets hit for a six. Then, you ask him to bowl the exact same delivery? Samiran was not able to do the math.

Sangharsh asked Samiran to trust him, as he knew exactly what he was doing. Samiran nodded reluctantly and started the run-up for his second delivery. It was indeed exactly the same as first one, and was driven straight right past the bowler for four.

Sangharsh said to himself, "Okay, good."

While coming back for his third delivery, Samiran sarcastically asked him, "Deewar *dekhi hai*? *Aaj khush to bahut hogey tum?* (Have you watched the movie *Deewar*? You must be very happy today?)"

Sangharsh smiled, put his arm around Samiran's shoulder and whispered: "Baazigar *dekhi hai?* (Have you watched the movie *Baazigar*?) Now listen carefully, champion. The batsman in all probability is expecting a short delivery from you, which means he is looking to play on the back foot across the line, around his waist level and at the pace of your first two deliveries. All you need to do is forget there is any batsman and aim at the bottom of the middle stump. And yes, deliver the fastest ball of your life."

After a brief pause, Sangharsh added, "Dilwale Dulhaniya Le Jaayenge (DDLJ) *dekhi hai?* (Have you watched *DDLJ*?)"

Samiran nodded as Sangharsh said, "*Ja Samiran ja, jee le apni zindagi!* (Go Samiran, go, live your life!)"

Samiran cracked up and started his run-up. As he reached the crease and jumped to deliver the ball, he saw the batsman's back foot in front of the bottom of middle stump, which he was aiming for. He hurled the ball with as much strength as he could garner. And then, as he was in his follow-through, he heard the most beautiful music a bowler could hope to hear—the sound of the rattling of stumps. He watched as the batsman limped back to the pavilion after falling prey to his deadly in-swinging yorker.

Samiran heard a growing roar from behind as Sangharsh ran towards him shouting, "*Jeeo mere SRK*! (May you live long, my SRK!)"

Once the key batsman was dismissed in the first over, Sangharsh's team got the initial advantage, the momentum of which was maintained. Samiran Ratan Kundu bowled with his tail up and ripped the opponent apart. The opposition was restricted to a score that was easily surpassed by Sangharsh's team and they won the Silver Plate for Ethal Bank.

While lifting the cup, Sangharsh wished Tanaya was there to witness the event.

10. Moving Forward

In a few months' time, Anuradha was promoted and she moved on to another role. She was replaced by Patrick. Apart from being great at his work, Patrick was a serious 'quizzard' ('quiz wizard'). Sangharsh and Patrick instantly hit off because Sangharsh would contribute to, and benefit from, Patrick's repertoire of trivia and questions. Patrick was so good that he had even won a car in a quiz competition.

Exchange of trivia and quiz questions led Patrick to believe that Sangharsh was a good quizzard too. So, he recommended Sangharsh's name for inter-corporate quiz competitions whenever he himself couldn't take part. Sangharsh participated—and lost. Always. He felt awful for letting Patrick and the bank down.

Patrick was brought in to take over from Anuradha and to head a new asset business segment. A team had to be built from scratch for this. Sangharsh was the first member to be picked for the new team, and he was made 'Assistant Manager'.

The moment he got his new visiting cards, Sangharsh was enthralled. It was the first time ever he had seen his name and the word 'Manager' on a globally respected bank's visiting card.

The first person he thought of was Tanaya but did not call her to give the news. He did not want to appear like a fool again. Since they were a part of the same group of friends, she would get to know of it eventually.

She did come to know of it, and called Sangharsh to congratulate him. The tone in which she spoke conveyed three messages in one:

I am really happy for you;

Don't even think about it; and

You are still not mature enough.

How women could convey mixed feelings from two ends of the spectrum in a single sentence remained a mystery to Sangharsh. However, he gave himself some credit for comprehending the tone—which he had been incapable of earlier.

Within the first few months, Sangharsh became the leading contributor of business in the country, and maintained his lead for subsequent months.

And then another opportunity knocked. A vacancy cropped up in the International Trade Department for the position of 'Manager'—two notches above Sangharsh's current position. Soumitra, the person holding the position, was moving to a different department, and his boss, Manmit, who had just joined the bank, had agreed to let him go on the condition that he find a suitable replacement. Soumitra was a senior employee with the bank and captain of the bank's cricket team. Sangharsh was in Soumitra's good books.

Before speaking to Sangharsh, Soumitra met up with two people.

First, he went to Patrick and said, "I am moving to another department and I want to recommend Sangharsh as my replacement."

Patrick's instant reaction was, "Forget it, he is the country's best performer and I cannot risk putting my targets at stake to fuel your ambitions."

"Patrick, let's not be myopic here. With this move, Sangharsh will get a double promotion. How many managers do you know who have given their team members a double promotion? Plus, it will be a good career move for Sangharsh," Soumitra argued.

"Hmm… I would need to speak with our Country Head before committing to anything," Patrick said.

Soumitra left. After twenty minutes, he received a call from Patrick saying that the Country Head was okay with the move if it meant a double promotion for Sangharsh.

Soumitra then went over to his boss, Manmit, and told him that he had found a suitable replacement in Sangharsh.

"If I understand correctly, he doesn't have any relevant experience. He is an Assistant Manager. Also, he is just a graduate. Without any experience, without good educational background and being two positions below your designation, I don't think he is an ideal candidate," Manmit said, and added, "*Tu to kat lega. Mera aur is department ka kya hoga?* (You will go. What will happen to me and the department?)"

Soumitra was ready with his response: "I understand your concern, Manmit. I would have been as concerned if I was in your place. Now, keep me aside, as my opinions might sound colored to you. I request you to get feedback about Sangharsh from his current boss, previous boss and seniors from other departments with whom he has worked closely. They will be able to provide you with balanced views."

Manmit immediately made a few phone calls and met some seniors from other departments. After an hour, he told Soumitra that he wanted to interview Sangharsh.

Soumitra called Sangharsh and asked him to come over for an important discussion. Sangharsh thought it was about another cricket tournament and that Soumitra would want him to captain the team again due to the seniors' unavailability.

Sangharsh went over and sat across the desk.

"So, Sangharsh, would you like to take my place?" Soumitra asked.

Sangharsh did not think for even one moment that Soumitra could be talking about work. He thought that Soumitra was contemplating retiring from cricket, and was offering Sangharsh captaincy for all future matches/tournaments.

"Sure, why not? Thanks! But *dada*, there are other senior players who are much more talented than I am and have been eyeing captaincy for a long time. I would definitely take it up if you want me to. It is just that I don't know how to captain seniors who are far better compared to me. But no worries—you are there to guide me," Sangharsh said happily.

Soumitra put his right thumb and right index finger two inches apart, and said, "You are this close to getting dropped from the cricket team. I saw the scorecards of all the matches of the tournament. You were the accidental captain. We won because the team performed well. Others scored runs and took wickets. You were pathetic."

Sangharsh wanted to say that the reason the team had performed well was because he had studied the team, studied opponents, and set batting orders and bowling line-ups as per the team's and opponents' strengths and weaknesses, which he figured by working hard during his 'homework'. The *Don*, *Deewar*, *Baazigar* and *DDLJ* sequence came flooding back to him.

However, all he said was, "I am sorry, *dada*. If I have not been able to portray that my captaincy contributed in some way to the victory. It is completely my fault. I take full responsibility and I am willing to get dropped."

Soumitra smiled and said, "Now, listen carefully. I did not call you to discuss cricket. I am moving to another department and want to recommend your name as my replacement. You will need to appear for an interview with Manmit—believe me, it will not be easy."

By the time Soumitra finished, Sangharsh's eyes were larger than usual; his lips were parted and his throat was dry. He swallowed and said, "I don't know what to say. I am too overwhelmed. But I am not sure if my boss will let me go."

"What do you think I have done all these years? Only work and play cricket? I know a thing or two about how to swing things. I have already spoken with him," Soumitra boasted.

Sangharsh couldn't believe that he was being considered for a double promotion. Now that the opportunity had presented itself, he wanted to give it his best possible shot. He wanted to prepare for the interview, but didn't know how and what to prepare.

On the day of the interview, Manmit didn't know what to ask him, as he knew Sangharsh did not have any technical knowledge. All he could do was rely on the feedback he had received. They chatted for a bit about career aspirations, and then the interview ended. Sangharsh could not figure if he had been selected or not.

Sangharsh lived in suspense and anticipation every day. After about a week, he got a call from HR, congratulating him on his double promotion. Although it was not entirely unheard of, double promotions were rare. Sangharsh couldn't help but think of his student days, when he had struggled to get promoted from one class to the next. And now there he was, with a double promotion at one of the most respected banks in the world.

This time, he called Tanaya to break the news. He could sense that she was elated to learn of his success. This time, too, he did not bring up 'anything else'. By then, he had understood that such things couldn't be thrust upon anyone, irrespective of any development.

Sangharsh joined International Trade as 'Manager', but did not know what was in store for him.

"How many times are we going to teach you how it's done? If it continues like this, I am not sure about the fate of this department and yours," Manmit told Sangharsh.

Sangharsh struggled to get a hold on the subject. He stayed back late at work to go through written materials; he read study modules, took online sessions and looked at transaction documents but was unable to get a firm grip. He felt like he had been thrown into an ocean and didn't know how to swim.

Soumitra came to the rescue. During his handover, he took Sangharsh for meetings with clients so that Sangharsh would observe him and learn. Manmit also lent his support by handholding him through various deals to give him a sense of how transactions were done. Slowly, Sangharsh came up to speed.

Once he had settled in, he eyed further growth. If he could get a double promotion, survive a storm and reach the place he had, he could definitely go further.

After a few months, a separate vertical was created within International Trade. Sangharsh was asked to manage East India—he would now report to Dinaz, Country Head, who worked in the head office in Mumbai.

It was the first time ever that Sangharsh had had to report to a boss who was in a different location. Since the boss was not physically present, one's efforts are not visiblc and, hence, an entirely different set of skills come into play – 'remote perception management'.

Sangharsh wanted to grow—so, he tried to do all that appeared to be right for his growth.

During the weekly conference calls with Dinaz and her boss, Sunay (the super boss, and a very sharp Bengali gentleman) and managers handling the North, South and West, Sangharsh would take the initiative and led the discussions on various solutions he was providing for clients that could be replicated by others. He learnt from other regional heads and tried to replicate their ideas in East. Soon, Sangharsh made friends from all over India.

After a year or so, Sangharsh did not see much potential for growth in his current role in Calcutta, so he requested Dinaz to see if she could transfer him to a different, more challenging location. Dinaz kept it in mind. Soon, there was a vacancy in Mumbai, and Dinaz called Sangharsh.

"Sangharsh, I remember you wanted to move. There is a vacancy in Mumbai, which is same as your current role. Would you like to come here?" Dinaz asked him.

"Thanks, Dinaz. But what is the point in moving in the same role? Is there a chance of getting the position of Senior Manager?" Sangharsh asked.

"This position is for Manager level only. I cannot give you a Senior Manager designation for a role that is defined as 'Manager'," Dinaz clarified.

"Then, I don't think it makes sense for me to move. Moreover, Mumbai is twice as expensive as Calcutta, if not more. So, this move does not make sense, career-wise or financially," Sangharsh said.

"Okay, no problem. Let me see what I can do," Dinaz said and hung up.

Dinaz then went over to Sunay and said, "Sangharsh does not want to come to Mumbai as this is a parallel move. He says it does not make career or financial sense to move to a city that is twice as expensive."

"Speak with HR and see if we can give him a promotion and increment. I want him in Mumbai," Sunay said.

"I spoke with HR before coming to you. They cannot give a promotion as this role is defined as 'Manager' countrywide. And they cannot increase his salary now," Dinaz said.

After thinking for a few moments, Sunay said, "Ask Sangharsh to call me."

Dinaz called Sangharsh and asked him to speak with Sunay. Sangharsh went inside the conference room, put up the 'meeting in progress' sign, sat calmly and rehearsed his lines before calling.

"*Hello, boss. Kemon aachen? Kotha bola jaabey?* (Hello, boss. How are you? Is this a good time to talk?)"

"*Haan Sangharsh, bolo.* (Yes Sangharsh, tell me.)"

"*Dinaz amay bolechey aapnar shatey kotha boltey.* (Dinaz asked me to call you.)"

"*Haan, aami bolechilam boltey.* (Yes, I asked her to.)"

"*Bolun, boss.* (Tell me boss.)"

"Regarding your parallel move, we cannot give you a promotion or increment right now. But if you come here, the future can be very good. Chances of becoming an AVP soon are high. *Tui ekhon choley aay, baaki porey aami dekhey nebo.* (You come now; I will see later what best can be done.) And convey your decision to Dinaz. If you have any queries, call me."

Sunay meant: Come now. If you perform well, you will be promoted to Senior Manager. If you perform well then, you might become an AVP.

Sangharsh *thought* Sunay meant: Come now. Your next designation will be that of AVP.

After that phone call, Sangharsh's thoughts raced back to what Anuradha had said on the first day of his joining: "We hire from IIMs and other Tier 1 Business Schools like XLRI, FMS at AVP levels."

Sangharsh thus understood Sunay's words to mean: Come now, and you will soon be at par with people from IIMs.

He called Dinaz instantly to convey he would move to Mumbai at same level. He almost added that he would do so at a lesser salary if needed, but wisely refrained from doing so.

"*Shaadi kar le, fir jahan marzi chaley jaana. Akeley kahan rahega, kya khayega, Tu wahan rahega aur mera jee yahan jalega.* (Get married and then go wherever you want to. You will be alone—where will you live? What will you eat? You will be there and I will be worried here.)" Sangharsh's mother lectured him.

"*Koi upay nahi hai, aage badhna hai tow jana hai.* (There is no option; if I have to grow, I have to go.)" Sangharsh said.

So, a Calcutta boy landed in Mumbai, the city where dreams are fulfilled and shattered.

Sangharsh had no clue as to what Mumbai had in store for him. The city was so different from Calcutta—he could sense that time moved at a much faster pace in Mumbai.

At work, Sangharsh interacted with people of his department and other departments; he met up with seniors across various sections and verticals, some of whom knew him from Calcutta. He developed a good rapport with peers, accompanied juniors to meetings and assisted them in getting business. He made friends all around. He got to know the city slowly as well.

The biggest task for Sangharsh after landing in Mumbai was not getting used to work culture, getting business, getting to know people, networking or perception management—it was finding a house to live in!

According to Sangharsh, finding a house of one's liking in Mumbai was like finding a soulmate. If you were very lucky, you would find it fairly quickly. If not, then God help you, as you may never find it, or, worse, have to compromise. Sangharsh was very picky, and unwilling to compromise. He did not like any house even after days of hunting.

"Congratulate me, Kavya, for hitting a century today," Sangharsh said to his friend.

"Wow! That's pretty quick. You just reached Mumbai, and you started playing cricket and hit a century! Congrats!" Kavya said.

"*Arre*, not for cricket, *baba*. I saw the hundredth house today!" Sangharsh said.

"What? You are absolutely mad, Sangharsh. You are looking for a rental place or maybe even a Paying Guest. How can you be so picky?" Kavya said.

"You know that's me. Why question me when you already know the answer?" Sangharsh smiled.

Kavya and Sangharsh were good friends, and part of the large school group. Kavya had been living in Mumbai ever since she had graduated. When Sangharsh set out on his house-hunt, Kavya accompanied him to view a few houses. After thirty houses or so, she gave up—and rightly so, as Sangharsh would come up with weird reasons for not liking a place. For example, even if the house was nice, he would reject it because he saw beetel leaf stains in the elevator.

11. A Chance Meeting with an Angel

"Sometimes you meet someone and, before you know their name, before you know where they're from, you know that this person is going to mean something to you, sometime in the future."

–Unknown

That is exactly what happened one weekend afternoon—the very reason you are holding this book!

As Sangharsh waited on the pavement of Linking Road (a suburban street in Mumbai) for a property consultant to show up, he saw a girl standing a few feet away. She had the most beautiful face he had ever seen—it attracted him instantly. It was as if she had just removed her seraph wings to show her angelic face, which shone brightly. She had magical black eyes and long, flowing hair. Sangharsh's head automatically bowed down in respect, which was when he saw the silver shoes she was wearing. Yes, she definitely looked like an angel.

The moment he set eyes on her, something pleasantly strange happened to him—a warm, comforting current engulfed his entire body. His heart started to beat faster, as if trying to convey something urgently. For the first time in his life, he experienced such a feeling. He could not comprehend what was happening and went into a trance. Then destiny played its part—she walked across to him and said, "Excuse me, I seem to have locked myself out of my car. The keys are still inside. I saw a police van go by and wanted to stop it to seek help. Then I saw a towing vehicle go past; I thought of stopping that, too, but they went away before I could act."

Sangharsh was transported back to reality, which appeared to be better than where he was—she was talking to him! After a few moments, he gathered himself and said, "You know there is a foolproof way of ensuring that you never get locked out of your car."

"Really? What is it?"

"Make a habit of locking car door with the keys."

"Aah, yes…That makes sense. Thanks!"

"By the way, your idea of stopping the police van and the tow vehicle was awesome. I wouldn't have thought of that. Let me see what can be done," he said.

Sangharsh scanned the periphery around and, within a few seconds, spotted a key maker right across the street. The shop had a huge banner that said, 'Car Key Remote Repair and New Key'.

Sangharsh thought, 'How come she didn't spot that?'

He asked her to wait beside the car and hopped across to fetch the locksmith.

"*Wo car dekh rahe ho uss paar? Uske andar chaabi reh gayi hai. Gaadi kholni hai.* (Can you see that car across the street? The keys are inside and the car needs to be opened.)"

"*Ho jaayga saab.* (It can be done, sir.)"

"*Kitne paise loge?* (How much will you charge?)"

"Sow rupye saab. (Hundred rupees, sir.)"

"*Achcha ye lo.* (Okay. Here it is.)"

Sangharsh returned to her with the locksmith. While the car was being worked upon, she took out her visiting card and gave it to Sangharsh.

The card read:

Advika Mehta

Designer. Planner. Consultant.

The aesthetic design of the card instantly appealed to Sangharsh. It had her address, phone number and email id on it.

"That's a beautiful card," he said.

"Thanks! It's a designer's card—it ought to be good," she smiled.

By then the locksmith had opened the car. "*Ho gaya saab.* (It's done, sir.)"

Advika asked him, "*Kitna hua?* (How much?)"

"*Saab ne paise de diye, madam.* (Sir has already paid.)"

"Why did you pay for it?" Advika asked Sangharsh.

"It's okay. You can pay me back by treating me to coffee some time at a place of my choice," Sangharsh said cheekily.

"Okay, cool," Advika smiled.

"So, you owe me coffee for the interest-free hundred bucks I lent you. I have your address, and I will send you an invoice for same," Sangharsh said.

"Ha ha! Yes, sure!" Advika smiled, got into the car and drove off.

Sangharsh kept gazing at the car till it became a dot and merged with the horizon. And then he stood on his toes to look for it a little more. It was gone.

Sangharsh was reeling heavily under the effect of meeting Advika. He stood there, thinking about the last few minutes of his life. How could a stranger, someone you met for just a few minutes, have such an effect? No logic held good. His head was spinning. He looked at the card she had given for a long time, saved her number on his cell phone, removed his wallet from his pocket and put the card safely inside—forever.

Then, he did some number crunching in his head:

Number of women he would have set eyes on until now since birth: One quingentillion (10^{1503})

Number of women he would have found beautiful: One million

Number of women he would have been attracted to: One hundred

Number of women who made him feel the way he felt now: One.

He deeply thought about Tanaya and tried to analyze their relationship, break-up and his desperation to get back to her—if that was that, what was this? Even more mysterious was the fact that he knew Tanaya very well. In this case, he didn't know her at all, except for maybe the magical 'three' words now.

Sangharsh wondered about how he could become a part of Advika's life in whichever way possible. He just wanted to stay connected with her.

But:

He didn't know how to win over a girl

And…

12. The Karmic Promise

Sangharsh started to email and text Advika almost every day. He never got a reply from her on email but she replied to his SMSes quickly. Each time he saw her name on the screen, his heart skipped a beat. He sent her trivia on various topics, which she liked very much; she even complimented him on his knowledge. He was elated!

At work, it was as if Sangharsh had renewed energy. He was in a sustained positive trance, which gave him power to work with heightened passion.

Tanvi, Sangharsh's colleague, a sharp, intelligent girl, who had become his good friend, noticed the change in him and commented, "How come you are glowing nowadays, with an extra spring or two in your steps?"

"Tanvi, I think I experienced something that many people have only read or heard about, but only a few fortunate ones have experienced," Sangharsh said.

"Have you fallen in love?" Tanvi smiled.

"At first sight. And I cannot take my mind off her," Sangharsh calmly replied.

Tanvi laughed and said, "There is no love at first sight; there's only lust at first sight. Is she very beautiful?"

"Yes, she is. But she is not the only beautiful girl I have seen. I have seen enough and more. She is different from all others—she's like an angel," Sangharsh said, his hand placed over his heart.

"Give it a few days' time—it will fade away. If it doesn't in a few days or weeks, or maybe a few months, I will believe in what you are saying about 'first sight'," Tanvi said.

"I know it will not fade away," Sangharsh said confidently.

"We will see," Tanvi challenged him.

In the meantime, Dinaz had moved into another role and was replaced by Amar, who was new to the organization.

Amar was a very knowledgeable, spiritually inclined person. He was a 'life hacker', and seemed to have solutions for any and every issue. As part of the handover process, Dinaz gave him feedback about the entire team and introduced him to important department/country heads across verticals.

After the handover was completed, Amar called Sangharsh for a meeting.

"I am not happy with you, Sangharsh," Amar said.

Sangharsh wondered, 'He has just joined. He has not worked with me yet, and doesn't know me. I am pretty confident about the feedback Dinaz or others would have given about me. What could it be?'

"Why Amar? What did I do?" Sangharsh asked, puzzled.

Amar flashed a broad grin and said, "Every Department or Country Head I met, when I asked how I could help, each one, either seriously or jokingly said, 'Give me Sangharsh.' What is it that you do? How do you communicate with them?"

Sangharsh smiled and said, "All I can say is that I just do what I say and say what I do. I conduct myself the way I am. I do whatever comes naturally to me."

"I like that answer. Well done. Keep up the good work and do not go anywhere else," Amar said.

Sangharsh was always thinking about Advika while working, and he performed better than ever. After a few days, Sunay asked him to go over to HR to discuss his promotion.

Sangharsh thought, 'The moment has arrived.'

"So Sangharsh, congratulations! You have been recommended for the role of Senior Manager. That was pretty quick, considering you just moved to Mumbai just a while back," the HR Manager, Kirti, said.

Sangharsh became visibly upset and his face went pale.

"Isn't it supposed to be AVP?" Sangharsh asked.

"Well, no, this role is for a Senior Manager only," Kirti said.

"Well, I will not take it," Sangharsh announced.

"What? For the first time in my career, I am seeing someone refuse a promotion. But why?" Kirti asked.

"Because I will take a double promotion," Sangharsh said.

"I have your HR record in front of me. Your last move was a double promotion. And you want it again?" Kirti said, surprised.

"That's the reason I made a parallel move to Mumbai from Calcutta. And that too, without any hike in salary," Sangharsh replied.

"Well, then, I am afraid I cannot do much at the moment," Kirti said.

"No worries. I understand," Sangharsh said and left.

He went over to Sunay and told him about what had unfolded with HR.

"What? You refused a promotion?" Sunay asked.

"Yes, boss, because I remembered your words that I will have a chance of becoming an AVP after coming here. *Ekhon ki korbo bolun*? (What should I do now?)," Sangharsh asked.

"*Arre*, that will always be step-wise, *baba. Aage Senior Manager taar por AVP* (First Senior Manager and then AVP)," Sunay explained.

Sangharsh immediately figured that he had misunderstood what Sunay had said. He had thought that if a double promotion could happen once, it could happen again. It was a gross judgment error on his part. He thought deeply for a while and then chose his words very carefully. "Boss, Amar had a meeting with me the other day. *O bolchilo je all Department/Country heads amake oder team ey chaiche.* (He was saying that all Department/Country heads want me in their team.) I am sure if you speak to any of them, they will gladly take me at the AVP level. Please guide me as to which role would be better suited for my career advancement."

Sunay thought for a while and said, "Let me see what can be done. And please ask Amar to see me now."

Amar met Sunay in the conference room.

"Amar, Sangharsh was telling me that other departments want him," Sunay said.

"Yes, Sunay. During Dinaz's handover to me, whoever she introduce me to, they all mentioned Sangharsh and wanted to have him in their team," Amar said.

"Now, he is aware of it and knows he's got bargaining power. He wants a double promotion again, or else we will lose him to some other department," Sunay said.

"Oh. I didn't realize things would take this turn. I thought mentioning that fact would motivate him to work even better—and his performance has improved over the last few days." Amar did not know that the reason behind Sangharsh's improved performance was something else.

"Whatever is done is done. We cannot let him go to any other department as that will reflect poorly on our ability to retain talent," Sunay said.

"I see. What do you suggest?" Amar asked.

"We will discuss that later. Now, listen very carefully. On a different note, I will approve hiring of three new head-counts in Mumbai for formation of a new team, and we will call for internal applications for a position that will manage this team. We will define this new position as a leadership role, which will warrant an AVP designation. And then, from all the applications received, we will interview and pick the best suitable candidate. Understood?" Sunay explained.

"Okay. Got it," Amar winked.

Sangharsh, who didn't know what was being cooked up, was depressed about not getting an AVP role. He wondered if he had done the right thing by rejecting the Senior Manager position.

He casually started to enquire with different departments regarding AVP vacancies and was pleasantly surprised to learn that even if there weren't any, people were willing to create a new position for him. He got an instant offer too.

"Amar, I have an offer for an AVP position from another department," Sangharsh told Amar.

"Okay. Is that an individual role or a leadership one?" Amar asked.

"It is an individual role," Sangharsh said.

"Okay. We are floating a vacancy in our department for a leadership role for an AVP position. Why don't you apply and see what happens?" Amar advised.

Sangharsh always wanted to get into a leadership role, as he knew that leadership was the only way to grow to the highest level.

The vacancy was floated; Sangharsh applied. Candidates were interviewed and Sangharsh was selected. Now, he had two offers in hand for an AVP position. While it was a no-brainer for him to choose the leadership role—that too, in the same department where he had a foothold—he still asked for Amar's advice.

"I leave it to you to decide. But remember one thing—think for a hundred times, a thousand times or maybe even more before taking a decision, but never even once after," Amar wised.

"Thanks, Amar. I will take the leadership role," Sangharsh said.

"Well, that was pretty quick. It seems you didn't even think about it twice, let alone hundreds and thousands of times!" Amar said.

"Yes, Amar. It's actually a no-brainer," Sangharsh smiled.

"I thought as much, but I wanted you to take the final call," Amar said.

"You always knew that I would get this role. Why didn't you tell me?" Sangharsh asked.

"For one, I always knew you had a strong chance of getting it. And two, always under-commit and over-achieve. It builds your credibility," Amar said.

Sangharsh raised his eyebrows and smiled.

And there he stood—a plain B.Com graduate with miserable marks, earning two double promotions in a row, at one of the most sought-after banking giants in the world. He was now on par with IIM graduates.

Sangharsh did not mention any of this to Advika. He felt his connection with her was at a different level, much beyond the materialistic and manipulative world around.

Sangharsh was now faced with the task of recruiting three people for his team. He interviewed many and hired three bright boys.

After a few days, Amar introduced him to another person as his fourth reportee—a summer intern from IIM–Ahmedabad.

Sangharsh couldn't help but think about the days when he so desperately wanted to get into IIM, but could not due to his academic limitations. Now, here he was—a boss to someone from IIM–Ahmedabad, arguably the best business school in the country. The very thought gave him goosebumps.

One evening, the country's business head sent an email to Sangharsh. It read: *Congratulations, Sangharsh! As a reward for your excellent performance, you have been selected to attend a convention in Zurich, Switzerland.*

Sangharsh couldn't believe what he read. Even though he loved travelling, he had never set foot outside India. This would be his first trip abroad. He was thrilled!

He took out his cell phone to write to Advika and ask her what he could get her from Switzerland. Before he started to type out the message, he received a text from her. It was the first time he had received an SMS not as a reply but as a start. His heart skipped two beats—but what he read brought his world crashing down.

Look, I don't mean to be rude or anything, but I don't think we should communicate further. I will meet you in my next life.

Sangharsh stood there, staring at his cell phone. He was completely shattered. He fought back his tears and typed slowly with shaking hands: *That's what you promised in our last life. Please keep your promise in the next life at least.*

By the time he pressed the 'Send' button, he couldn't see the screen properly—it had become moist.

That was the day he experienced two extreme emotions within a few minutes of each other. Extreme happiness at being selected for the Swiss convention, and then extreme sadness after reading Advika's text.

While Sangharsh believed in past lives and the journey of a soul as one that lived through many lives—each life for learning and advancement of the soul—he now wondered if it was better to follow the school of thought that advocated only one life.

With faint hope, he thought of a quote by Gabrielle Zevin: *"Someday, we'll run into each other again, I know it. Maybe I'll be older and smarter and just plain better. If that happens, that's when I'll deserve you…"*

13. One Swiss Cow, Please

"Hello, Thakur! Main Switzerland aa raha hoon. (I am coming to Switzerland.)" Sangharsh called Akshay, a very close school friend.

"*Arre waah! Hamare saath nahi rukey tow Shweta aur main wapas jaane nahi denge. Kavya bhi soch rahi hai aane ka.* (If you do not stay with us, Shweta and I will not let you go back. Kavya is also thinking about coming.)" Akshay spoke from Basel, Switzerland.

Shweta, Akshay, Kavya and Sangharsh and many others, including Tanaya, were part of the same group of school friends. Shweta and Akshay had been in a relationship since school days; they eventually married and settled down in Switzerland. The guys of the group addressed each other as 'Thakur'.

"*Wapas nahi jaane diya to achcha hai. Saari zindagi Switzerland mein rahunga!* (If you guys do not let me go back, it is good. I will get to live in Switzerland all my life!)" Sangharsh joked.

"Ha ha! Jokes apart, tell me your plans," Akshay said.

"I need to attend a convention in Zurich for three days, then I am off to the UK for a holiday, after that I will come back to Switzerland and stay with you guys," Sangharsh said.

"Good deal. Give me the dates and I will plan our itinerary accordingly. Cheers!" Akshay said.

Sangharsh hung up and made another call.

"Bhai, main Switzerland aa raha hoon. (Brother, I am coming to Switzerland.)" Sangharsh was speaking to Raghav, who lived in Lausanne.

Raghav and Sangharsh went back a long way—they had been batch mates at the IT course. Raghav was the brightest of the lot and Sangharsh was the dullest, yet they were great buddies.

"*Fantastic! Mere saath rukna padega.* (You have to stay with me.)" Raghav said.

"*Haan zaroor rukunga bhai.* (Yes, I will definitely stay, bro.)" Sangharsh said. He continued, "I have a convention to attend and then I will be in the UK for a while. I will come back to Switzerland to stay with another set of friends at Basel. After that, I will come visit you."

"Great! Cool! Let me know the dates," Raghav said.

Sangharsh then spoke to Kavya. She was thrilled to learn that Sangharsh was going to Switzerland. She was planning to go there too and then to France and Germany with Shweta and Akshay. She insisted that Sangharsh join her. He wanted to but he only had visas to Switzerland and the UK, and not a Schengen visa that allowed entry to other European countries (Switzerland was not a part of Schengen in 2008).

And then, for the first time ever in his life, Sangharsh landed on foreign soil. The sight of the countryside landscapes made his jaw drop—undulating green meadows romanced with the horizon, punctuated with brown cottages with sloping roofs scattered all around. Grazing cows with tinkling bells around their necks. It was as if someone had painted the sceneries by hand—it seemed perfect! While he had seen such places in movies and photographs, witnessing the same in person was quite a different experience altogether. However, after three days, the same picturesque sceneries seemed boring—effect of the law of diminishing marginal utility.

After the convention got over, Sangharsh took off from Zurich and landed in gloomy, overcast and wet London.

As Sangharsh passed the immigration check-point, he saw his bags pass through the X-ray machine. As that happened, two uniformed security officers briskly walked towards him, pointed their fingers at him and shouted, "Enemy, enemy, enemy," Sangharsh froze. Did they spot something untoward in his baggage? Did someone slip something into his bags without his knowledge? What would happen now? Would they interrogate him? Whom could he call for help? So many permutations and combinations went through his brain in under ten seconds. He started sweating profusely.

The officers realized that they had scared him enough and broke into laughter as one of them said, "Look at your jacket—it's from our enemy's team."

Sangharsh realized that he was wearing a Manchester United jacket. He did not follow soccer much but he was able to understand that this entire episode could have been avoided if he had worn a Chelsea or an Arsenal jacket.

He heaved a sigh of relief and said to himself, "Welcome to Great Britain."

"Excuse me, do you have accommodation available for a single person?" Sangharsh asked the girl manning the reception at a youth hostel.

"Let me check…you are in luck—we just have one bed available in a mixed dorm of four," she said.

"What is a mixed dorm?" Sangharsh asked.

"It is a room with two bunk beds; it is called 'mixed' because it is for both women and men."

Sangharsh thought, 'Wow! I will get to share a room with multiple women. Super!'

Without revealing his enthusiasm, he said, "Okay. If that is the only option available, I will take it."

When he checked in, there was no one else in the room. It was late evening. He thought, 'The girl at the reception said only one bed was available. Where are the women?' After fifteen minutes, he heard a knock on the door. He went to open it and couldn't believe what he saw—three gorgeous women walked in. All of them looked like super-models. They were extremely friendly and introduced themselves to Sangharsh. They were from Sweden.

Sangharsh sat on his bed, legs folded, and looked on as the girls settled in, put on make-up, got ready and left within minutes. Sangharsh was left sitting on his bed, legs folded, cursing his luck.

The next morning, as Sangharsh was stepping out, the girls walked in and went to bed. It was as if they were saying, "You and me are continents apart."

After travelling solo for a few days in England and Scotland, Sangharsh went back to Zurich. Shweta, Kavya and Akshay received him at the airport.

"Welcome! Or, should I say, welcome back!" Shweta greeted. "We are expecting another friend to land in a few minutes. Let's wait for a while and we will all go together," she added.

In the meantime, Sangharsh narrated how his UK trip had been, why he did not like London and how he had fallen in love with Edinburgh. He spoke about his tour of the 'mecca' of cricket and tennis—Lords and Wimbledon. He narrated his other experiences, including the security officers' humour at immigration and Swedish rendezvous.

"Yay! The flight has landed!" Kavya exclaimed, pointing towards the sea of passengers trickling in.

All of them looked towards the arrival gate. Kavya, Shweta and Akshay almost ran forward. Sangharsh stood there, frozen. It was Tanaya!

Sangharsh battled several thoughts in his head. He was seeing Tanaya after ages. He felt numb. What happened to the feelings he had for her? What about the insurmountable pain of break-up he nursed for so long? What about the desperate need to get back together? Why didn't he feel the way he felt before?

He thought to himself, 'Maybe the answer to these questions are in my wallet.'

Akshay looked at Sangharsh and winked. Sangharsh smiled back hesitantly and greeted Tanaya, who was surprised to see him. Kavya, Shweta and Akshay looked at each other and smiled expectantly.

Tanaya's plan to visit Switzerland had been made before Sangharsh's, and she hadn't known that Sangharsh would be there. It was a coincidence that their dates had clashed. Or was it just a coincidence? Or did this have to happen for Sangharsh to get final clarity from himself on where he stood?

"Let's go," Akshay announced.

"I need to get a local SIM card before we go," Sangharsh said.

Sangharsh got a Swiss SIM card and inserted it into his phone, and then Shweta drove everyone to Basel.

As they passed through the Swiss countryside, Kavya and Tanaya were awestruck by the beautiful landscape. Sangharsh had seen similar picturesque views only a few days earlier, so he was not as interested. Moreover, he had something very important to do.

Sangharsh took out his cell phone, opened the 'Write Message' window, keyed in '*Hi'* and sent the message to Advika. He hoped she would respond upon realizing that the message was not from India, and yet from someone she may know.

Sure enough, pat came her reply: *Hi. Who's this?*

This is someone you know. I am in Switzerland right now and will be back in Mumbai in a few days. What can I get for you from here?

But I need to know who you are.

Am sorry, that's a surprise. I cannot tell you who I am. You will get to know once I reach India. Be patient ya. Tell me what can I get for you from here.

Babbal, if this is you, I will kill you.

What kind of a silly name is Babbal?

Ok, get me a couture dress from Paris.

Unfortunately, I don't have Schengen Visa and I will not be going to France. I will be in Switzerland only. In future, when I visit Paris, I will get you a couture dress.

If you are not kidding, get me a Swiss cow.

Ok done! Swiss cow it is for you!

Sangharsh was extremely happy to establish contact with Advika again, but at the same time wondered if Advika would stop all communication once she knew who it was.

Sangharsh thought for a while, then turned to Akshay and asked, "Thakur, is it possible for me to join you guys in Paris? Can a visa for an Indian national be arranged from Switzerland?"

"No. You need to apply for a French Schengen visa from India only. You should have done it before coming here. Anyway, Tanaya has also got only a Swiss Visa. Both of you enjoy Switzerland while we are away," Akshay smiled wryly and winked at Shweta.

Sangharsh thought for a few moments and said, "I would have loved to but I need to visit another friend in Lausanne. I have given him my word."

"For Paris, you would have skipped Lausanne. So, skip it now," Kavya butted in.

"No. In that case, I would have gone to Paris and then to Lausanne, while you guys would have carried on to Germany," Sangharsh clarified.

"But why suddenly Paris? And only Paris?" Shweta asked suspiciously.

Sangharsh knew that if he as much breathed a word about why he really wanted to go, they would pin him down and extract all the details. So, he just said, "I have a fickle mind. Very unpredictable."

"No, you don't. We know you better than that. Tell us the reason," Shweta prodded.

"What happens if you break the speed limit on a Swiss highway, Shweta?" Sangharsh changed the topic.

"Then you pay a fine that is commensurate to your income. Recently, the son of a furniture giant broke the speed limit in his Ferrari and had to pay 200,000 Swiss francs as fine. When I broke it some days ago, it was a few hundred francs. But we clearly understand that you wanted to change the topic. You are such a fiercely private guy," Shweta caught Sangharsh.

They spent the next three days travelling within Switzerland, but Sangharsh did not text Advika even once. He was content with the prospect of taking something back to her. He feared that if he communicated further, he might blow whatever chances he had created.

The day Kavya, Shweta and Akshay left for Paris, they again asked Sangharsh to stay back with Tanaya. Sangharsh refused the suggestion and left for Lausanne to visit Raghav.

Tanaya was alone. Sangharsh felt sorry for her.

After spending a couple of days with Raghav, Sangharsh went to Zurich Airport one night before the scheduled departure of his flight. He needed enough time for 'shopping'. He scanned all the shops for the best 'Swiss cow' he could get. Finally, he got a Swiss cow souvenir toy; a soft toy shaped like a Swiss cow that made a 'moo' sound when its toes were pressed; a cowbell; and chocolates for Advika.

Sangharsh landed in Mumbai, went home, took out Advika's gifts and rushed to a courier company to send her the present. He kept calling the courier company every few minutes to ask if the 'parcel' had reached. Finally, around evening, he got a confirmation that it was delivered. Advika would know that the gifts were from Sangharsh by looking at the sender's name.

Sangharsh instantly texted her asking if she liked what he sent. He did not get a reply. Next day he tried calling her but could not connect. The phone was unreachable. He tried calling every hour, then every day for many days, but could not get through. He searched for her on the web too, but couldn't find her. He was shattered—again.

At work, his performance deteriorated; he couldn't focus even if he wanted to. He found it hard to concentrate.

He had a very talented team but their performance suffered because of him.

"What's wrong with you, Sangharsh? You don't seem to be 'there'," Amar asked him.

"Nothing, Amar. Everything is okay," Sangharsh lied.

"I love the passion with which you work, Sangharsh. Somehow that seems to have been dampened over the last few days. Look, you might be having personal issues. Let me know if I can be of any help," Amar said.

"Thanks, Amar. I really appreciate your support. I have learnt a lot from you about leadership and otherwise as well. I have also noticed that you are somewhat partial towards me when compared to my peers. Why is that?" Sangharsh asked.

"You know, Shakespeare once said: 'What you are shouts so loudly in my ears I cannot hear what you say'," Amar said.

Sangharsh tried to hold back but couldn't and said: "Right. But Shakespeare didn't say that. Ralph Waldo Emerson did."

"Could be. But the meaning is not lost," Amar smiled.

"Right, Amar. Could I ask you a favor, please? If I may?"

"Yes, sure."

"Can you please ask for my transfer back to Calcutta or somewhere else? I don't seem to be adjusting well in Mumbai."

"Running away from your problems is not the solution. Fight it. If you cannot, for whatever external reasons, then fight it from inside yourself. You are letting your issues get the better of you. You should strive for a life where, even if everything is stripped off you, you should be at peace. It's all in the mind."

"Wow! How do I do that?"

"Meditation. For a change, instead of your body, take your mind for a holiday."

Sangharsh took that advice a little too seriously, did some research and took to meditation.

It seemed to work for him. He began to feel relaxed and at peace. However, the desire to be connected to Advika did not fade. Every few days, he called her but to no avail.

Once, while meditating, Sangharsh went into a deep trance and his thoughts took him to what looked like his past life. He saw himself standing with a person who seemed to be his wife.

He looked more intently and found that she had a conspicuous scar, in the form of a small cross, on the top of her left foot. They were fighting over something and she left him. He could not see much, but he could tell that it was not Advika. He came out of the trance and reassured himself that it could not have been Advika, because she had promised him in her last life that they would be united in this one.

Sangharsh missed Advika terribly, and wondered at the marvel of it all. He had met her just once in his life, and that too only for a few minutes. Yet, she had had such a strong effect on him. Even though she ended all communication with him, he was not able to subdue his thoughts about her.

More than a year went by. He told Tanvi, "Remember that 'love at first sight' discussion we had?"

"Yes, 'lust at first sight' discussion," Tanvi laughed.

"It's been more than a year and it has still not faded."

"What? You can't be serious!"

"I am. I still cannot take her off my mind."

"Have you told her?"

"I cannot reach her anymore. Her phone has been unreachable for more than a year now."

"Go to her house. If I remember correctly, you had her visiting card and it had her home address."

"I still have it with me. It's been in my wallet ever since."

"So, go to her house, stupid!"

"And say what? 'I don't know you, you don't know me, but I am in love with you?' And get thrown out? No way. I cannot risk that!"

"Keep hoping for a miracle then. You are mad!"

14. 'Something' Has Changed

The next year, Shweta and Akshay visited Mumbai. All of them gathered at a friend's place. Akshay took Sangharsh to a separate room, closed the door and asked him, "Why are you not getting married to Tanaya? We all know she wants to marry you."

Sangharsh said, "For one, she has not told me anything. And truth be told, even if she does, my answer will be 'no'—because I know I will not be able to do justice to her anymore. I will not be able to keep her happy."

"Why is that? You guys were in a relationship earlier. You know each other well. And we all know how badly you wanted to get back to her. Do you like someone else? What has changed now?"

Sangharsh flirted with the idea of removing Advika's card from his wallet and putting his finger on it, but he merely said, "I cannot put a finger on any one thing, at least not for now."

Akshay did not catch the last bit. Sangharsh thanked his stars that Shweta was not there.

After a while, Shweta and Kavya had a similar discussion with Sangharsh. He repeated what he had told Akshay, except for the last bit.

Ever since Advika had left his life, Sangharsh wanted to leave Mumbai. Then, an opportunity sprung up in Calcutta. A new position was announced for the position of Vice President and Regional Head, East India. Sangharsh leapt at it and was the first one to apply.

He wasn't surprised to learn that he had been selected. On the day he got the congratulatory mail from HR, he went blank.

He experienced a sense of emptiness inside him. He could not decipher that feeling. Was he feeing empty because he had surpassed even some of the IIM graduates and reached a level where he could not have imagined during his student days or early on in his career? Or was he feeling empty because he would be leaving the city where he had experienced '*Veni, Vidi, Amavi*'?

In 2010, Amar moved to another country and Sangharsh headed back to familiar territory, carrying with him loads of experience, everlasting friendships, some maturity, a relatively relaxed mind, a broken heart and a visiting card. He travelled as much as he could, always with the card. Every now and then, he tried to call Advika, but never reached her.

The pressure to get married was increasing. A lot of his friends were married, and some even had kids. Alliances kept flowing in, but Sangharsh always excused himself.

"*Kya kami hai isme? Achche khandaan se hai. Sundar hai, padhi likhkhi hai. Kyun mana kar raha hai?* (What is her shortcoming? She is from a good family, beautiful, educated. Why are you saying no?)" Sangharsh's mother would ask him upon seeing his lack of interest.

"*Kami kisi mein nahi hoti. Aur sab mein hoti hai. Wo tow padhi likhi bhi hai. Aur sundar bhi. Main na padha likha, na sundar. Tow waise dekha jay tow kami mujhme hai. Usme nahi. Lekin mujhe lagta hai ki shaadi ke liye kamiyaan ya gunn nahi giney jaaney chahiye. Jodion ka mel hona chahiye. Aur mujhe nahi lagta ke hamara mel thik hai.* (No one has any shortcomings. And everyone has shortcomings. She is educated. And also pretty. I am neither educated nor good looking. So, in a way, I have shortcomings, not her. But I think marriages should not be based on counts of shortcomings or skills. It should be based on compatibility. And I don't think we are a good match.)" Sangharsh would respond. The conversation was repeated as if on a loop every time an alliance came in.

Sangharsh did not want to get married because his friends were married. He did not want to get married because his younger siblings were married. He did not want to get married because his family wanted him to. He did not want to get married because of societal pressure. He did not want to get married because he was getting old. He wanted to get married only after falling in love.

He feared that Advika had gotten married and left the city, maybe even the country. The thought hurt him, but there was nothing he could do except to pray for her happiness and wellbeing, which he always did. And wait to fall in love again. Was that possible? He did not know, but he waited nonetheless.

In the meantime, Sangharsh got attracted to a select few women, whom he thought were on the same wavelength as him, but, somehow, he never felt the way he had in Advika's presence. He never proposed the idea of a relationship to anyone. He could sense that there were some who wanted to be with him—some proposed as well—but he didn't reciprocate because he did not fall in love the way he fell in love with Advika.

Sangharsh worked, travelled, meditated and played sports. He did not come across anyone whom he wanted to spend the rest of his life with.

15. Carte Blanche

In the beginning of 2012, Ethal Bank underwent a global restructuring exercise and Sangharsh got a call from the central HR team.

"Hi, Sangharsh. How is it going, buddy?" asked the HR head.

"All well, captain. How can I help you?" Sangharsh replied.

"Sangharsh, we are undertaking a global restructuring procedure. As a result of this, your position in East India will be redundant in the next three months. It is a relatively small region and we do not need such a senior resource there. You will need to see if there are other positions available elsewhere, internally or externally. Let me know if I can be of any assistance."

"Oh, okay. Thanks for keeping me posted. Let me think through this and I will get back to you."

Sangharsh was shaken after the conversation. He had spent almost a decade in the organization. He could see that the things he had given his life to were breaking apart. He called Amit, his current boss in Mumbai.

"Amit, I just got a call from HR regarding…"

Amit cut him off: "Yes, I am aware. There could be a position in Mumbai—while your designation will be the same as current, the work profile will be that of something junior than your current role. Would you want to consider it?"

Sangharsh thought for a while and said, "Am afraid not, Amit. Not Mumbai. And definitely not a junior role after heading a region."

"Hmm…I thought as much. Let me see if any other leadership role can be managed elsewhere. In the meantime, you also keep looking."

Sangharsh searched for a position—internally and externally—but did not get the kind of job profile he was looking for.

Sangharsh had been toying with the idea of starting his own consultancy in international trade and finance for some time. With the positive response customers had been giving him on his international trade structuring transactions, Sangharsh had thought of doing it on his own. Maybe this was a sign for him to go after what he had been planning. He stopped looking for jobs and turned his focus to setting up the infrastructure for starting his own consultancy firm.

Sangharsh started to look out for office spaces and finalised one even before leaving Ethal Bank. His last day at Ethal Bank and the first day at his own firm were less than 24 hours apart. He felt a sense of freedom that he did not even know existed. After working for so many years in a constrained environment, having a space of his own came as a huge relief.

As soon as the paperwork regarding the formation of the firm was complete, Sangharsh opened his mailbox, clicked on 'Compose' and wrote:

Dear Ms. Advika Mehta

We are a financial consultancy start-up firm and we were wondering if you could assist us with designing our logo, which would be used on visiting cards, letterheads and brochures.

Do let me know how to take this forward.

Looking forward to hearing from you soon.

Thanks.

Regards,

Sangharsh Vashisht

He did not get any response. The email did not bounce back.

Within a month of starting his own business, Sangharsh received a call from Dinaz. "Hi Sangharsh, if you are still looking for a job, I have a VP-level leadership role in Calcutta in a different vertical for you. Would you like to join?"

This was a very tempting, lucrative offer. Sangharsh thought for a while and said, "Thank you, Dinaz. I am very grateful to you for thinking of me. However, I have just started my own consultancy business and I don't think I will be doing justice to myself if I give it up without trying. I have just jumped off a cliff and am building an aircraft on my way down. Grabbing a parachute at this point is no fun," Sangharsh reasoned.

"Good! I like your spirit! Let me know if I can be of any help. All the best!" Dinaz said.

A few days into his business, Sangharsh came across a childhood friend, who, along with his wife, was doing a similar kind of consultancy—they specialized in domestic financing, while Sangharsh had expertise in international trade financing. After a few rounds of strategic meetings, they decided to join hands and offer a full gamut of services for clients from Sangharsh's office. The couple was very talented with good product knowledge and had valuable network of senior ex-bankers to assist in concluding deals.

Sangharsh's firm was converted into a private limited company. However, within a few months, Sangharsh realized that they all had extremely different opinions. Things were not working out the way they had envisaged. The partnership broke and Sangharsh closed down his office. He took a few days off for a meditative break and came back with fresh perspectives.

Sangharsh floated another firm individually and went back to doing business by himself again. He formed strategic and economic tie-ups with banks, financial companies and multi-nationals for mutually beneficial business exchanges.

His work entailed travel all over India—especially to Mumbai. Every once in a while, he tried to call Advika but never got through. Although he knew he was trying in vain, he would still call to check. His absolute last resort was to pay a visit to the address given on the card but he could not think of a valid practical reason to go there.

One fine day, Sangharsh received a wedding invitation that made him really happy—it was for Tanaya's wedding. He was relieved to learn that she found someone who she could spend the rest of her life with. He attended the wedding and wished the newly wedded couple a lifetime of happiness and togetherness. He felt light—very light.

In the meantime, Sangharsh's family gave up on their hopes to see him get married. He met girls through friends, acquaintances, dating applications, matrimonial sites, but 'the bell never rang'. He decided to wait for someone who would make him feel the way Advika did, something akin to what Amitabh Bachchan had said in the movie *Amar Akbar Anthony*:

Jise dekh kar man ka violin automatic bajne ko chalu ho jaay. (On seeing her, the heart's violin should play automatically.)

Dimag ka ghanti bajne lage. (The mind's bell should ring.)

He waited.

16. Blast from the Past (?)

"What's he on?" Olivia asked.

"Nothing. He doesn't drink," Anu said.

"Smoked up?"

"Never had a single cigarette all his life. And he is a vegetarian."

"What? How can someone dance like that without being high on anything?"

It was New Year's eve. Sangharsh had made it to the party this year after several unfulfilled invitations from his friend, Anu.

Olivia was Anu's friend. She had a dusky complexion with sharp features and looked as if she seldom skipped her exercise regime. She appeared to be charming and amiable. Sangharsh had noticed her the moment he stepped into the party; the very sight of her evoked mixed sensations in him.

"So, Mr Dancer! What are you doing at a party where booze is flowing freely, people are smoking up and food is mostly non-vegetarian? Hi, I am Olivia," Olivia smiled and introduced herself to Sangharsh.

"Ah, interesting name! And it is even more interesting that you are calling me a 'dancer' when you can clearly see I have two left feet! I dance to the music. 'If music be the food of love, play on!' I am sorry, I had to say it after knowing your name. Hi, I am Sangharsh," he smiled.

"Ha ha! No worries! I get that sometimes. So, you dance because you are looking for love, is it?" Olivia teased him.

"Well, 'Love sought is good, but giv'n unsought is better'. Sorry again, I couldn't resist myself. But, I promise, that was the last quote. That's because I don't know any more," Sangharsh laughed.

"Ha ha! I have not got that from anyone yet. Are you a literature student by any chance?"

"Far from it. Never been a good student. But yes, I am a student of life!"

"So, tell me, what have you learnt from life?"

"Ah…If I had known I would be tested, I would have done some last-minute studying before getting here—just like I used to do during my schooldays."

"Ha ha! No, seriously, I am curious. What has life taught you?"

"I told you I am a student of life, never told you I am a good one. So, just like in school, I didn't learn much here as well."

"Ha ha ha! You are funny. But you have lots to learn, it seems!" Just then, Olivia's boyfriend arrived and she went away with him.

The moment Olivia went away, Sangharsh felt a knot in his stomach. It was a strange feeling—a part of him couldn't wait to meet her again and another part did not want to see her again.

Sangharsh ignored the feeling and went back to dancing. He did not see her again that evening.

Among the sea of New Year messages Sangharsh received was a text from a very close friend, Shree, who believed that they were 'soul siblings'. Sangharsh believed that, at any given point in time, she always knew 'n+1', where 'n' was equal to the number of things in the universe. A part of the text read: *Hope you find* THE ONE *this year.* Over their more-than-twenty-years of friendship, that was the only time she had texted something like this. The '+1' was being put to test.

About a week later, at a coffee shop:

"You think I never went to school or what?" Olivia asked Sangharsh.

"Why? What happened?" Sangharsh asked, even though he knew why she said that.

"Even I have never heard of these," Anu added.

Sangharsh looked at them and proclaimed, "In today's day and age, you have Google at your arm's length disposal. At the touch of a button, you can check if I am right or not. And, if you want, I can tell you the meaning of these as well," Sangharsh said.

"Okay, tell us while I google them," Olivia jumped.

"*Qi* is a Chinese life force. *Xi* is the fourteenth letter of the Greek alphabet. *Za* is the short form of pizza. *Xu* is Vietnamese currency. And these are all perfectly acceptable words in a game of Scrabble across the world," Sangharsh announced.

"Yaaaaa! You are right! These words do exist! Wow! I think we should totally get married. Our children will turn out to be so smart!" Olivia joked.

Even though Sangharsh knew it was meant to be a joke, he felt slightly uneasy, but just laughed and said, "Let's order some 'Za' slices and we shall pay with Indian 'Xu'!"

A strange sensation engulfed Sangharsh when he was in Olivia's presence—he was attracted to her but he also didn't want to be beside her.

Suddenly, Olivia looked at Sangharsh and said, "Are you a girl?"

"Now, where did that come from?" Sangharsh was taken aback.

"Look at your hands. They look manicured! I am sure your feet would be pedicured, too. Show me," Olivia demanded.

Sangharsh removed his feet from under the table and took off his slippers.

"See! I told you. You have such nice feet and you are still unmarried!" Olivia exclaimed.

"Only once in my life did I get a manicure and pedicure—only as a trial—and that was ages ago. I don't even remember when. And how is marriage related to feet? Are you saying that whenever I propose to someone, I should say 'Look at my feet and marry me'? I am sure I will get a stern reply—'My foot'!"

"Ha ha ha! I am a girl. Look at my feet and look at yours." Olivia removed her feet from below the table and took off her shoes.

The moment Sangharsh saw Olivia's feet, he became visibly disoriented. He tried to act normal but the damage was done.

"Now come on, it's not that bad," Olivia smiled.

Sangharsh smiled hesitantly and murmured: "It's good. In fact, it's better than mine. You are just being kind."

They resumed their game of Scrabble, fought and googled a few more words. After a while, Anu left and Sangharsh drove Olivia to her home. On the way Olivia asked, "What happened? You looked upset back there. We noticed."

"Nothing…A work-related issue suddenly cropped up in my head," Sangharsh lied.

"Don't lie… We both know it was not work related. Anyway, if you choose not to tell me, it's okay. If there is something I can help you with, let me know," Olivia offered.

"Thanks. I will seek your help for sure if need be," Sangharsh said.

Olivia received a call on her phone. After hanging up, she told Sangharsh, "That was my friend, Aditi. She is a very good tarot card reader. If you want to consult her any time, let me know."

"Okay, sure. Text her number to me and I will get in touch with her if required," Sangharsh said.

Sangharsh dropped Olivia off. While he drove home, parts of what Olivia had said ever since they had first met kept playing in his head:

You are looking for love is it?

So tell me, what have you learnt from life?

You have lots to learn it seems.

I think we should get married.

Olivia's words echoed in his head in a loop. He just couldn't take his mind off what he had seen that evening—a scar in the form a small cross on her left foot.

Did she mean: *Did you find your love in this life or not?*

Did she mean: *Has your soul progressed with experiences from past life and this life?*

Did she mean: *Do you want me to help you in this life in any way?*

It seemed Olivia had come into Sangharsh's life to help him in whatever way she could. Sangharsh was drawn to her more but the strange feeling remained. He was utterly confused.

By the time Sangharsh reached home, Olivia had sent him the tarot card reader's number. Even though Sangharsh had never tried this earlier, he called Aditi, fixed an appointment and went over the next day.

"How can I help you?" Aditi asked him.

"I don't know where to start. But whatever we discuss needs to be kept confidential," Sangharsh said.

"Don't worry. It's a part of our professional code of conduct. Whatever we discuss remains between us only. I know my friend has referred you, but be rest assured, it is not going out anywhere," Aditi said.

"I am extremely confused about something in my life. About a girl. I cannot get clarity in my head," Sangharsh said.

"Who is she? What's her name?" Aditi asked.

"Well, she is your friend, Olivia."

"Ah, I see. So, what is the confusion? Do you think she is your soul mate?"

"No. I don't think she is my soul mate. If that was the case, I wouldn't have been confused. I cannot explain the feeling. I want her beside me, yet I don't want her to be with me."

"Is there any specific question you have in mind?"

"Yes. Can you please tell me if she was my wife in my past life?"

"Okay. Wait"

Aditi shuffled a pack of cards and then drew a few. She read them and said, "Yes, she is from your past life."

Sangharsh was stunned.

"Any other question?" Aditi asked.

"Okay. I get a feeling that she wants to help me in whatever way she can. Can you please check if I can help her in any way?" Sangharsh asked.

Aditi nodded, shuffled the cards and drew out some.

"No. I am afraid you will not be able to help her in any way," Aditi said.

Sangharsh asked a few other questions but he was not really interested. He was also not sure whether to take such things seriously. He wondered if Olivia had felt something similar as well.

They met that evening.

"I need to tell you something, Olivia," Sangharsh began.

"What is it? How was the meeting with Aditi?"

"In fact, I wanted to discuss that."

"Tell me."

"Ever since we met, I have had this strange pull-and-push feeling for you, something I cannot explain. At the risk of sounding absolutely weird, impractical and illogical, I think you were my wife in one of my past lives. And your friend, Aditi, also confirmed this fact. I was wondering if it is just me or if you also felt something just as weird?"

"Ha ha ha! What? I was your wife? Did I look the same?"

"Yes! You looked like a movie star—and you look just as good now. Happy?"

"Ha ha ha! Well, wife or not, I don't know. And yes, it's just you. I am already in a relationship with someone. These things did not occur to me at all."

"Ah. I thought I would run it past you to figure if you are as weird as I am. Turns out you are normal—the way it's supposed to be—unlike me!"

"Ha ha ha! You know you are completely mad, right?" Olivia laughed.

Sangharsh felt relieved.

17. The Right 'Connection'

"Well, look who I ran into," crowed Coincidence.
"Please," flirted Fate, "this was meant to be."
–Joseph Gordon-Levitt, Musings: The Tiny Book of Tiny Stories

Sangharsh's work in Mumbai expanded and he had to shift his base from Calcutta to Mumbai again for at least six months and depending on work, could be more than that also. It would be his second innings. He secretly hoped that Advika did not remember the tip he had given her on how to never get locked out of a car—he hoped he would again bump into her after seven long years on a street, with the keys stuck inside her car.

"The way you are so picky for even a rented place, how on earth will you be able to find a girl to spend the rest of your life with? I seriously think that you are actually looking for a girl from your previous life. Otherwise, who in his sane mind would go through 200 houses? And the last time round, you saw some 100-odd places if I am not mistaken!" exclaimed a friend.

"This time, it is 205. Last time, it was 125," Sangharsh said.

"And a girl? Found one yet? When will you get married?"

"Maybe never—if I never find THE ONE. And perhaps you are right. I just might be looking for someone from my previous life."

"*Koi iska ilaaj karao re bhai!* (Someone please get him cured!)"

Out of the 205 houses Sangharsh saw, he picked one. If he had picked any of the other 204 houses, he wouldn't have had to look for an interior designer. It was the only unfurnished house he had liked, which needed to be done up by a professional interior designer. Again, hoping against hope, he tried calling Advika knowing fairly well that he would not get through. And he did not. Sangharsh then got in touch with a few designers whom he found on the Internet. Some went to his house, took measurements and gave him quotations. He went to a few furniture stores as well to see in-house designers, but he did not want to take a liking to any. He felt the time had come to pay Advika a proper visit.

Before taking the final step, Sangharsh thought of making one more attempt to find Advika. He conducted a personalized search on Google. He typed 'Interior Designer Advika Mehta'. A suggestion popped up but the spelling was incorrect. He hit the link and reached a website that showed her name with the correct spelling. However, the home page said that they were going through some changes and would be back soon. Another page on the same site had her contact details and her photograph. Sangharsh did not recognize her in the picture, but the moment he saw the photo, his heart skipped a beat. Perhaps the reason he did not recognize her was because when he had first seen her seven years back—the only time he had seen her, his heart, not his eyes, had 'seen'. This time also, his heart shouted out.

'There's got to be some serious metaphysics playing here', he thought. The people we meet are the ones we invite in our lives to serve some purpose—either for some good experience(s) or for some learning(s). Did she unknowingly invite him into her life to honor her promise? Or did she invite him for some other purpose? Maybe both. Maybe neither. However, he was still not a hundred percent sure that it was her.

He called the number mentioned on the website. She answered the call. The moment Sangharsh heard her voice, he felt a relaxing sensation engulf him from head to toe. Her voice was magically comforting. Instantly, as if due to a reflex action,

Sangharsh gripped the phone warmly with both hands. He gathered his composure and narrated his requirement in a 'non-affected' way, all the while wondering if she was THE ONE. She told him that she would not be able to assist him as he wanted only a part of the house to be done up and she only took on full-scale renovations—breaking down everything and doing it up entirely in a new way. However, she suggested someone who could help. Sangharsh thanked her, disconnected the call and again wondered if he had gotten the right 'connection'.

It was then he decided that, if she turned out to be THE ONE—irrespective of the final outcome—he would write a book. One freak meeting more than seven years ago, a few days of interaction and then no communication. He just couldn't forget her and finally found her after seven years. This called for at least a book if not a movie!

He called up the reference given by Advika and requested the person to come over to have a look at his house. The designer saw the place and took measurements. When he was about to leave, Sangharsh asked him, "Are you in touch with Advika? Does she still live in Bandra 18th road?"

"Well, we are not in touch often, but I think she lives in 16th road," he replied.

"Oh. Are you sure?" Sangharsh asked, fearing that Advika could have gotten married and moved to another place.

"No, I am not completely sure."

"Okay. No worries."

Sangharsh messaged Advika and discussed design-related possibilities. He wondered how he would ask her if she was THE ONE. He sent her some snaps he had taken on his holiday, which she found 'gorgeous' and 'just amazing'. After a few days of text exchanges, he messaged her and said that he'd felt a sense of déjà vu while interacting with her and asked if she was by any chance from Bandra 18th road. She did not respond. After a few days of not getting a reply, Sangharsh removed her visiting card from his wallet, clicked a picture from his cell phone and texted her.

Is this you?

His heart skipped a beat when he saw Advika's name on the screen. She wrote: *Oh my God! Where did you even find this? I had forgotten about this.*

What???? So this is you????

This was probably the first time he had used more than one question mark while asking a question to someone. This time he used four—twice.

Yes.

Did you recognize me?

No.

Sorry about the condition of the card. It's been seven-odd years.

I can't believe you have it. I had forgotten about this card.

And I still can't believe it's you. Am thinking of putting this up at Sotheby's for auction!

Ha ha.

That was the first time he had made her laugh. That laugh seemed to send a message to him—that she wanted him to make her laugh more. Sangharsh always prayed for Advika's happiness, and now he had a chance to be a part of it by making her happy. He couldn't he happier! He took up the self-designated assignment, and hoped it to last for a lifetime, and beyond. At the same time, Sangharsh was skeptical, as he didn't know if Advika was single or not. There was one more thing he was very skeptical about.

He still didn't know how to win over a girl.

Sangharsh just could not believe that he found THE ONE after seven long years. He took out 'soul sibling' Shree's text about finding THE ONE and read it again and again. Now the only thing left was for Advika to 'find' him. For the next two days he didn't know how to react and what to say. He was reeling under happiness—a sense of intoxication seemed to have overtaken him.

After two days, he sent her a message: *It's been in my wallet for the past seven and a half years. Wallets have changed but this remained constant. I will send you the bill for safekeeping. :)*

Ha ha ha. Where did you meet me? Lol. And my number is the old one. This is so strange. Lol.

Ha ha! Yes. Very, very strange! Straight out of a fiction book. I am thinking of meeting a few Bollywood directors to narrate the story and ask them to make a movie on this. :)

Ha ha ha ha. So weird. I had forgotten that card. Imagine.

Seriously? All the more strange! Seven and a half years is a long, long time…

Ha ha ha. I went to study after that. So my life is divided into before Italy and after Italy.

Sangharsh was doing great on his assignment—she had laughed five times within an hour! However, her last sentence made him shiver and gave him goosebumps. He remembered her last text more than seven years ago as if it was yesterday: *I will meet you in my next life.* He couldn't help but think again about her unconsciously inviting him to honor her 'promise'. Her going abroad for studies explained why he never got through to her number.

After a couple of days, Sangharsh texted her: *You have no idea how freaked out I am. Much more than you are coz: a) I remember what happened seven years ago and b) Something you said then and something you said now has a very uncanny connection. Absolutely unreal. Am thinking whether to write a book on this or to make a movie. :)*

When did we meet? I have no idea. What did I say then?

Honestly I don't know how to put it across…I guess I need to narrate the script to you first! :)

Ha ha ha. Okay.

It was at this point that Sangharsh's idea of writing a book started to take shape. He began recollecting the chain of events that had led him to this crossroad. He got in touch with publishers to check if his book could get published. He thought of a working title: *The Silver Shoes.*

After starting to write and receiving positive feedback from the publisher, Sangharsh took printout of the title page and texted the picture to Advika.

The script is underway! :)

What!!!! Ha ha ha. What is this? What shoes?

Silver shoes are the magical shoes that appear in the 'Wizard of Oz'. It is said that the shoes can transport the wearer anywhere they wish. And when we met for the first time, you were wearing silver shoes. Do you even remember those shoes or you have forgotten them, like your card? :)

Really? I don't own silver shoes. Oh my God. You sure it's me?

100%. Otherwise, how could I have gotten that card? And when I tell you in detail, you will remember—am pretty sure. Lost memories will come flooding back :)

I have a very bad memory. Almost amnesia.

You are lucky! A French philosopher once said that key to happiness is nothing more than good health and bad memory. :)

Aha ha ha. I love by that.

Sangharsh knew pretty well that Advika wanted to type 'live', and that 'love' was a typographical error. He also knew that such errors were committed from the conscious mind. It could very well have been a 'Freudian Slip'. And Master Oogway's statement—"There are no accidents"—wasn't made without a purpose. He wanted to stay with that 'love' for as long as he could.

After making some progress with the manuscript, Sangharsh asked Advika if they could meet so that he could narrate everything about their first 'accidental' meeting. She didn't want to meet—and rightly so, as she did not know him. According to her, someone suddenly told her that he knew her from seven years ago and wanted to meet up now. She found the whole thing very 'sketchy'. He told her about how he had gotten her number—and she accused him of 'web-stalking'. That hurt him badly, and he told her so. He then narrated to her the story of how they met, but only after extracting a promise from Advika that she would design his house layout. She agreed.

After Sangharsh narrated the story, Advika said that she remembered the car incident and Sangharsh's gifts from Switzerland. The day the gifts had arrived, she was on her way out to go to another friend's house. It was a huge package and her parents had wondered what it was and who had sent it. She opened the package at her friend's place. There, she met another friend for the first time and gave one of her gifts to him—the small cow soft toy that made a 'moo' sound when its toes was pressed. That friend, a world traveller, still carried it with him. She also mentioned that even though she had a bad memory, she remembered the car incident because, whenever she met that friend, they brought up the 'toy' topic and her only connect with that friend was that toy.

Within the span of one minute, she mentioned 'toy' thrice but wrongly typed 'you' instead of 'toy' all three times. In their conversation, spanning over two months, Sangharsh had spotted just two typographical errors by her—the first one was 'love' and the second one was 'you'.

Sangharsh was interpreting everything from a different, maybe impractical level, but he was happy to decipher what he did. He wrote: *Ha ha ha! See. I found so much more material for my book now, :)*

Advika replied: *Exactly.*

Sangharsh couldn't help but smile from ear to ear and then burst into laughter knowing very well that she was definitely not seeing what he was seeing. He obviously didn't tell her what he was reading because she did not mean from a conscious level what he was thinking. Sangharsh wondered if what he was thinking could be right at any level or not.

He asked her: *Do you still have the other cow?*

She replied: *No. Aye the chocolates though.*

He had not asked her about chocolates, but she had mentioned it and made her third typographical error—she wrote 'Aye' instead of 'Ate'.

Just when Sangharsh felt he had gotten after seven years what he was looking for—'Love You'—he had wondered whether what he was thinking was right at any level. There she was, driving home the point by saying 'Aye' (Yes).

Even though Sangharsh knew what 'Freudian Slip' meant, he still googled its exact definition. It read: 'An unintentional error regarded as revealing subconscious feelings.'

Sangharsh knew he was being childish in deciphering these messages in an impractical way, but he still did so because he did not want to just put the thought aside without savouring it. He closed his eyes and felt bliss for a minute. He was reminded of Al Pacino's dialogue from *Scent of a Woman*: "Some people live a lifetime in a minute."

Sangharsh had lived a lifetime in that minute.

From that moment onwards, thoughts about Advika occupied Sangharsh's mind. Wherever he went, he imagined Advika with him. Beside him in the car, at the movies, while dining with friends, even in the middle of business meetings. He was living the Lionel Richie number, 'Stuck on you', quite literally.

The book progressed at a rapid pace. He stole time whenever he could between his work schedule to write. He wrote on flights, wrote late into the nights, and wrote while taking bites. He became somewhat unsocial. He did not tell anyone that he was writing a book. Only the publisher and Advika knew about it.

Sangharsh travelled quite often. Once, when he was in Calcutta, he texted Advika and asked if he could get her something. She said, *No*, to which Sangharsh replied, *C'mon ya… It's not the first time I will be getting something for you. :)*

Ha ha ha ha. True. So it's my turn.

The very thought of Advika gifting him something was more than enough for him, who was already truly and madly in love with her, to make him fall in love all over again.

He reminded her that she had increased her deliverables from one to two. The first deliverable was to make a design plan of his house, and the second was the gift she had just mentioned. Sangharsh began to think of what gift he would ask for. He then jogged his memory to the time Advika had asked him to get a cow. Sangharsh wondered if she remembered what her first demand had been. So he asked her: *I know it's difficult to recall, but do you remember that the Swiss cow was the second thing you wanted?*

I wanted a cow??

Yes! I got the Swiss cow because you had asked for it without knowing that it was me. I was texting you from a Swiss number, so you could only guess that it was someone from Europe. The cow was the second thing. Now, what was the first thing?

You know I must have said it as a joke. I'm sure I thought my friends were playing a prank.

Exactly. You wrote, 'Babbal if this is you I will kill you.' :) Then you wrote, 'If you are not kidding then get me a Swiss cow.' :)

You remember a lot I must say…

Then she got busy and said would chat 'late'—then immediately corrected it to 'later'. Little did they both know that it would actually be 'late' and not 'later'—perhaps as 'late' as it would take for the entire book to be written.

After a couple of days, Sangharsh wrote to her: *Just like nature maintains ecological balance, similarly, for every person that has amnesia, there is someone who remembers a little more!*

He did not get a reply.

Sangharsh's memory was actually not good at all. He made phone calls to people but forgot whom he had called—he had to remove the phone from his ear for a split second to look at the screen. He did not remember the major milestones of his life; he needed to look at documents to figure out when certain important events happened. He still told Advika jokingly that his memory was only good when it came to her.

After two more days of not getting any reply, he wrote, *Hey I am sorry ya…*, hoping she would laugh it off and ask why. He did not get a reply.

Sangharsh assumed he had screwed up big time by joking about amnesia—it had probably upset Advika. He was willing to go to any length to apologise. And that was the beginning of his (unknowing) journey of self-sabotaging any chances he hoped he had created.

Sangharsh thought the best way to apologise was to send her flowers with a note saying 'Sorry'. Not just any flowers—it had to be thought through. He researched on appropriate flowers used for apologies.

He called up florists across Mumbai to check if they had white tulips, blue hyacinths and white orchids. White tulips and blue hyacinths were not available anywhere. White orchids were available at some places. He went to multiple places to look at options for the best possible white orchids along with an appropriate instrument to hold the flowers. The entire package needed serious thought—it had to be something relevant to the reason why an apology was being sought. After visiting several florists, Sangharsh finally selected one where he found white orchids and something to hold those flowers—a fishbowl. He had the bouquet made in front of him to check how the final package looked like. After multiple attempts, he settled on a particular look—that was the best he could do with his limited aesthetic and design sense. After all, it would go to a designer—a very special one!

Once the bouquet was ready, Sangharsh gave the florist Advika's office address which was mentioned on her website and her contact number, and requested him to transport it with utmost care. He also stressed that he be informed the moment it was delivered. It was estimated that the flowers would be delivered in about an hour's time.

Sangharsh called the florist before the hour was up to check on the delivery. He was told that the delivery guy had reached at the given address and called Advika, who asked him to deliver the same to another office address as they had moved. The florist gave the new address to Sangharsh. At the alternate address, the florist was told to deliver the bouquet to another location in Bandra 18th road. Sangharsh immediately understood that Advika called the flowers at home. It was the same address as on the card he had been carrying. It was a possible indication that she was not married. He became hopeful.

After a while, he received a text from her. *You sent me flowers?*

As he was about to reply, he got a call from her. His heart skipped several beats; before he could gather his wits, the phone stopped ringing. Sangharsh composed himself and called her. He did not anticipate what he heard from the other side.

"You sent me flowers?"

Sangharsh sensed trouble when he heard her stern tone.

"Hey! Yes, I did. Did you like it?"

"You have put me in an awkward situation. Why did you send flowers?"

"Oh. I am sorry. I thought I had goofed up and wanted to apologise. You were not responding to my messages."

"What goof up? And I did not respond because I got busy. Without knowing anything, you sent flowers to my residence. You could have told me you were sending them."

"I am terribly sorry. I did not realize that it would cause so much trouble for you."

"Look, we met only once for a few minutes many years back. I don't know you. I wish you all the best for the book you are writing, and I will help you with that, but don't expect anything else. Nothing else. Okay? Are we cool?"

"Yes, cool. And I am sorry once again."

She ended the call. Sangharsh returned to the message window where he was about to write to her. He saw her 'online' there and wondered if she was also looking at his window on her phone. He wanted to write so much at that point that he went completely blank and could not write anything.

Sangharsh was shattered. Again. He had sabotaged his chances by sending her flowers. He wondered if, at some level, he had unconsciously pushed her away from his life, whereas, in reality, he was even ready to take a bullet for her. Was it because he had become so used to not being in relationship for such a long time—more than fourteen years—that some part of him felt that his freedom was being threatened? Or was it because his unconscious was trying to protect him from a possible heart-breaking eventuality?

Did his unconscious make him act that way so that he would push her away? Or was the time not right yet? He took full responsibility for this situation and was willing to fight it out. She was worth surrendering his freedom to, even at the risk of getting hurt again. This, he was very confident about, without even knowing her—only because he was answering his heart's call. He was usually very particular and picky about everything—especially when it came to the people in his personal life. He was fiercely guarded. He wouldn't let people in easily. He had enough and more close friends in all parts of the world. At any given hour on the clock, he could pick up the phone and call so many people at even at 3 am (their time). He was extremely thankful for this priceless gift. He was willing to surrender his freedom or whatever it took to be with someone who was a complete stranger. This definitely was a part of reality that science hadn't caught up with yet.

The lines from the song 'The Scientist' by Coldplay kept playing in his head:

Come up to meet you

Tell you am sorry

You don't know how lovely you are

I had to find you

Tell you I need you

Tell you I set you apart…

…I was just guessing

At numbers and figures

Pulling the puzzles apart

Questions of science

Science and progress

Could not speak as loud as my heart

After more than a week of not hearing from Advika, Sangharsh wrote to her and explained the rationale behind what he had sent:

There were twenty-one white orchids in the fishbowl. White orchids stand for apologies. I wrote regarding your 'amnesia', which I thought didn't go down too well with you. Still, I shouldn't have sent those flowers and I am terribly sorry. Now that leaves me with twenty more mistakes to make.

Coming to the fishbowl. Why a fishbowl? Generally, goldfish reside in a fishbowl. There is a popular belief that goldfish have a three-second memory and every lap of the fishbowl is like seeing the world for the first time—which is why they never appear bored. This is a myth—goldfish have a much longer memory span. It was an attempt to project to you that what you think regarding your memory is also a myth. You too have a memory span of more than three seconds.

I am not too worried about the forgetting part, but have I been forgiven? :) I need help with the book.

Sangharsh hoped this would crack her up, but did not get any reply. In the meantime, he kept punching away at the keyboard and continued writing with whatever material he had. After two weeks of not getting any reply, he sent her six names—options for her character's name in the book—and asked her to pick one.

He still did not get any reply. After three more days, he again asked her for help with the book; he needed some feedback on the content and answers to a few, very important questions. So, he wrote:

There's no rush. Whenever you get time, please help me with the following:

1. *The day we first met—was that the first time ever that you got locked out of your car?*
2. *Did you ever get locked out of your car again after that day?*
3. *Did you follow the suggestion I gave you on how to never ever get locked out? Do you remember it now?*
4. *How many times in your life have you approached a complete stranger on the streets for some help? And gave your visiting card?*
5. *For your feedback, please give me your email address so that I can send you the pages I have written so far.*

He did not get any reply. Sangharsh wondered if she had asked herself these questions.

18. Signs from the Universe

Sangharsh grew uneasy over Advika's silence. Even though he meditated regularly, he could not remain centred. The lack of a response from Advika made him restless. He sought expert help with guided meditation. He searched on the Internet for places in Mumbai where he could get assistance. And where did one of the search results land him? To a place that was right in the building where Advika lived! What kind of a sign was that? On one hand, she was not communicating at all; on the other, Sangharsh was being led to her close proximity. Was she still subconsciously inviting him? He couldn't tell. Did he visit that place? Of course not. She had already accused him once of Web-stalking her; if he bumped into her in the building, she would recognize him by his display picture which she would have seen on the phone while messaging, she then might accuse him of physically stalking her. He was not willing to take that chance.

By not going there, did he (again) unknowingly push her away? Maybe.

Pratik, an investment banker in Mumbai and one of Sangharsh's childhood school friends, called him one day and asked if they could meet. Parts of Pratik's and Sangharsh's work were similar and they had been in touch over the phone to discuss business, but a meeting had never worked out. Sangharsh was back home from work and he didn't want to miss the chance of catching up with Pratik after many years. Pratik went over to Sangharsh's house.

Sangharsh greeted him by saying, "*Itney saalon baad fursat mil gayi tujhe? Kya piyega bol—wine, whiskey, vodka, rum, beer?* (You finally got time to meet after so many years? What will you have?)"

"*Arre! Tuney peena shuru kar diya?* (What! You have started drinking?)" Pratik was surprised.

"*Nahi. Main peeta nahi sirf pilata hoon. Ye stock iss jaise waqt ke liye banaya gaya hai.* (No. I don't drink. I only make others drink. This stock is for occasions like these.)"Sangharsh said.

"*Kya yaar. Itna bada ho gaya abhi bhi peena shuru nahi kiya? Bina kisi nashey ke kaise jeeta hai bhai?* (What? You are so grown up and still you don't drink? How do you survive without any addiction?)" Pratik teased him.

"It's not that I have never tasted. I have tried but never enjoyed; moreover, it's not healthy, so I stay away."

They chatted, discussed their good old school days and argued about why was Sangharsh was not married. Sangharsh stuck to the 'falling in love' theory while Pratik asked him to be practical. They compared life in Mumbai vs. Calcutta. For such discussions, Sangharsh always had a dialogue ready: "You can take a person out of Calcutta but you cannot take Calcutta out of a person." They joked, laughed and made group travel plans—knowing fully well it would never work out.

Some bottles of beer and a few glasses of cranberry juice later, they discussed business and agreed to visit each other's offices. Sangharsh asked Pratik for the exact location of his office. The moment Pratik mentioned the address, Sangharsh's eyes lit up—he couldn't believe what he just heard. Sangharsh then removed his cell phone, fiddled with it for a few seconds, handed it over to Pratik and asked, "Is this address and your address the same?"

Pratik looked at it and said, "Yes, it's the same address. Same building. Only the floors are different."

Sangharsh barely managed to contain his thoughts and emotions and remained as calm as he could while all sorts of thoughts rushed through his head.

It was the same building as Advika's office—the same place where she had asked for the flowers to be delivered.

After Pratik left, Sangharsh sat, aghast. He pushed the 'rewind' button in his head and closely linked the life events that had led him there—especially over the last few months. Hunting over 200 houses and finding the only one that needed designing. Then miraculously finding Advika. Then finding ways to make her laugh. Then unknowingly finding reasons to push her away. Then magically being led to where she lived. Then coincidentally being invited close to where she worked.

He wondered if, ultimately, all this would reach a sensible ending or not. But he was sure of at least getting closure.

As Sangharsh wrote the book, he was being wary of his literary skills—or rather, the lack of it. He always wondered if what he was writing would make sense or not. He wished he had someone to guide him. Then, one day, while he was typing away on his computer, he received a text from a friend who happened to be his neighbor as well—and she was an award-winning published author!

The text read: *One Day Workshop: I'm conducting a full day writing workshop that covers everything you need to know about writing and publishing. It's Mumbai's first such workshop. Do attend.*

Sangharsh instantly replied: *Count me in. And I can't believe the timing! Just perfect!*

She wrote: *Serendipity! Please do bring something you've written for review.*

That was exactly what the doctor had ordered. He attended the workshop and received a great deal of valuable tips on writing. He tried to incorporate his newfound knowledge as well as he could. At the time of review, when Sangharsh's work was read out, the author mentioned that the piece had lots of grammatical errors, but that the content was very interesting.

Other participants also felt an instant connection—so much so that, while exchanging contact details after the event, some people saved Sangharsh's number under the name of the book's main character.

Sangharsh hoped what he was writing would be liked by Advika—as, essentially, the book was being written for only one reader.

19. Unfinished Business

Despite Sangharsh's literary and creative limitations, he went out of his skin to write a whole book based on just one freak meeting—that too, more than seven years back. That was because destiny had brought Advika again into his life. Was he sabotaging his chances further by writing a book? Maybe. Perhaps that was the sure-shot way for her to decide not to be a part of his life. Why would she want to be with someone who was so below average? Someone who did not have a good academic background. Someone who neither looked good, nor talked wise. Someone who had failed at so many stages in his life. Places where he had somewhat succeeded could have been just accidental with some strokes of luck. Why would she want to be a part of his struggles? She had no reason to be with him—and, maybe, he was rubbing it in by writing a book.

However, Sangharsh was extremely grateful to Advika, as he was able to decipher some purposes Advika had served in his life—seven years back and also now. Back then, he had realized what it was like to fall in love at first sight—absolutely magical! And then he gained clarity on where he stood with Tanaya. Now, when Advika re-surfaced, he started believing in miracles. And she was the one, because of whom he would become a published author! Maybe there were other purposes she had served, and he was not able to identify those yet. Would she serve any more purpose(s)? Maybe.

Sangharsh wondered if his appearance in Advika's life served any purpose(s) for her? If it had, was she able to identify them? Would it serve some purpose(s) in future? He couldn't be sure.

Advika's main concern seemed to be the fact that she didn't know him. How could Sangharsh make her know him?

1. **By writing a book.** That was one of the reasons why he had started to write. However, after writing a few pages, he realized that this wasn't the best way for her to know him. After all, he was writing it, and he could write anything. He could project himself as a hero and get her to know him the way he wanted to. Doesn't work.
2. **Could people vouch for him?** Of course. Sangharsh wondered how many people could vouch for him. He took his cell phone, opened the 'Contacts' folder and started counting. The number crossed 100 and he was still on 'A'. Then he realized that this would also not work because she wouldn't know the people who would vouch for him. How could she trust them?
3. **Six-degrees-of-separation.** This concept is so pre-1990s. In today's day and age, six degrees would be reduced to perhaps four. And since both of them were in the same city, there was a very high possibility of maybe three or two degrees of separation. Could be even one. Sangharsh needed to get the people she knew and trusted to vouch for him. Could he do that? If it really came to that, then he would go to any extent and endeavour to reach out to the people she knew and trusted to seek information about her and vouch for him. But he did not believe in *"All's fair in love and war"*, he thought it would be unethical to go around asking about her without her knowledge. He would only do that if she wanted to '*know*' him that way.

Sangharsh knew that in some cases, even a lifetime of togetherness might not be enough to 'know' someone, and at times, only a few moments together could make a world of difference in 'knowing'. All he wanted was for Advika to spend some time with him and decide by herself. Under what circumstances she would *not* want to know him? There could be many (including not liking his face, which was very likely and he would respect that) but he could think of two major reasons—either she was married or in a 'loving' relationship with someone. In such cases, Sangharsh would be happy for her and pray for her happiness and wellbeing, like always. He would then return her visiting card that he had been carrying for *every single day*. Or there could be a third possibility—that she was in love with someone and was not able to be with him (just like Sangharsh himself). If that was the case, Sangharsh would go out of his way in whatever way possible within his capacity to help her. And if she was single, then he would like to conclude some 'unfinished business' with her.

Sangharsh took any agreement, whether fleetingly, jokingly or seriously between them as a promise—that's how agreements are supposed to be. The unfinished business was divided into three parts:

Part one: Promises from Sangharsh to Advika

Part two: Promises extracted by Sangharsh from Advika

Part three: Promises from Advika to Sangharsh

Part one: Promises from Sangharsh to Advika

1. "In future, whenever I visit Paris, I will get a couture dress for you." Sangharsh had written this to Advika from Switzerland. He visited France later in life, but did not go to Paris. Was this yet another coincidence? How many people from India visit France for a holiday and not go to Paris?
2. "I am thinking about whether to write a book on this or to make a movie." And there he was, slumped over

his computer for months together—EVERY SINGLE DAY—to honour this promise.

Part two: Promises extracted by Sangharsh from Advika

1. "You can pay me back by treating me to coffee some time at a place of my choice"—coffee for a hundred-rupee loan to unlock the car seven years back. Interest waived.
2. "Design Sangharsh's house layout." This promise was extracted by Sangharsh before he narrated to Advika how they had met seven years ago. This was the trickiest of the lot. It would be very difficult for Sangharsh to live in the house designed by Advika if she would not be a part of it. Still, as promised, he decided to get the design layout done, but she was not even willing to communicate with him. He hoped, someday, he would be able to make her honor this promise.

Part three: Promises from Advika to Sangharsh

1. "I will meet you in my next life"—her last text to Sangharsh seven years back. According to Advika, her life was divided into 'before Italy' and 'after Italy'. So, in a way, this was her next life. She did not promise anything else—she just said she would meet. And meeting even once would be sufficient to honor this promise.
2. "So it's my turn"—a gift for Sangharsh from Advika. Since Sangharsh had got what Advika wanted—a Swiss cow—it would be his 'turn' to ask for the gift.
3. "I will help you with the book." She had proactively mentioned she would help Sangharsh with the book he was writing. And it was the most important promise of all. Once the book would be completed, he would get

it printed and take it to Advika for her to read it and would request her to write the Epilogue. It would go for final printing and availability around the world only after Advika wrote the Epilogue—it would serve as a form of final closure for Sangharsh. His work in Mumbai was over and he was not required to live there anymore, however, he still stuck around to get the most important closure of his life.

The good news for Advika was that most of her promises could be honored within a matter of minutes. Advika could meet Sangharsh for coffee and present the gift to him. Then, the only promise remaining would be to write the Epilogue, which also she could write within a few minutes (or she could take as much time as she wanted).

What if she did not want to see him even once or ever again, even after reading the book? Sangharsh was absolutely okay with that. He would be happy with the thought that he did whatever he felt was the best he could do to win his love—it still might not have been enough for her—but it was the best he could think of and acted upon. He had absolved her of all her promises. She was absolutely free and need not think even once that she had to honor her promises. He now understood that a part of *real love* is complete freedom for the one you love.

There was a marked difference in Sangharsh's feelings when he started to write the book and when he was about to finish it. He was at peace now. How did that happen? Was it because all his feelings were channelled into writing and he was freed from the shackles of unexpressed love? Or was it that after a lot of soul searching, he realized that he was looking for love externally? What really could have happened when he saw Advika for the first time was that he had projected a part of self onto her and fell in love with himself? After all, it is all '*inside*'. With time, he also learnt that what really matters is being grateful for everything he had in his life and loving every moment without any thought of past or future and whenever the mind wanders, and it will, then being just a watcher, a witness and bringing the mind back to the present moment with love. And that's also where *real love* can be found. This learning and realization was enough for him to be at peace and he trusted the journey of his life.

What if Advika said "Yes"? Would Sangharsh then say "No"? Could that happen? Well, he didn't '*know*' her. If he said 'No' because he didn't 'know' her, would Advika then write a book?

Anything could happen. Sangharsh could leave Bombay and go back to Kolkata. Or, now that he would become a published author, he would walk with a swagger—with his collar pulled up and sleeves rolled, expecting to be surrounded by girls with whom he would paint the town in all hues of red. He would pick and choose the ones he would date and the ones he would reject.

But:

He still didn't know how to *patao* a girl.

However:

He now knew what *real love* was.

Epilogue